LIONESS OF GAZA

BY
Norman Jay Landerman-Moore

Table of Contents

Dedication

To those who fit, or strive to fit, the first part of that sage saying; "There are three kinds of people in the world. Those who make it happen. Those who watch it happen, and those who spend their lives wondering what happened!"

About the Author

Norm Landerman-Moore was born near Sacramento and raised in Southern and Northern California. He is the oldest of nine children and is descended from some of America's earliest families. He, along with seven High School friends, joined and served with the United States Marines during the Cold War.

Later, Norm received his undergraduate degree from the College of Environmental Design at California Polytechnic University and went on to graduate work in urban economics and Law.

After initial years of professional service in Land-Use Planning for planned communities and return from service with ARAMCO's Planning Division in Saudi Arabia, he received a Career Executive Appointment from Governor

Ronald Reagan as Chief Planner with the California State Resources Agency.

Later Norm founded a Strategic Planning firm, Landerman-Moore Associates, which served public agencies and private clients in the United States and abroad until 2010. Since retirement in the San Juan Islands, Norm immersed himself in genealogy. As a result of extensive family research, he began writing true accounts of ancestors which became the basis of creating three historical fiction novels, "Samuel of the Nations", "Jaded Horses", and "All But One".

Later, Norm expanded into fictional novels based, in part, on actual events and places, such as Where Pelicans Fly, and now, Lioness of Gaza. He is also researching and writing additional family history novels which are in progress. They include Quindaro, The Eighth Heaven, Mom, and Scribblings which will be published over the next few years.

Among several accomplishments, Norm is an experienced long-distance sailor. Twice, he crossed the North Pacific Ocean from Hawaii to Newport Beach, California in a fifty-foot sailboat. Of those experiences, Norm commented, "Out there, forces of nature reveal your limits!" … "You discover the reality that you are not invincible!"

INTRODUCTION

About twenty years had passed since the "Old Man", the German, and sailing companion of Tracey Schaffer, died. His ashes were spread in the Pacific Ocean at the opening of Cat Harbor, Catalina Island. Young Rowland Shaffer was a six-month-old baby then. At twenty years of age, he is exceptionally brilliant in studies and well into his third year at the University of Texas; advancing in computer technology and mathematics. *WANG, IBM,* and a new player in the scramble for technologies called *MICROSOFT* have headhunters tracking his progress.

Rowland's father, Tracey Shaffer, is a leading commercial and industrial real estate advisor, and broker, with offices in five counties of Southern California. Rowland's mom, Elsje, of the well-known, wealthy, and influential Dutch Van Steenwijk family, owners of Van Steenwijk Inter-Island Shipping of Jakarta, Sumatra, Seri Lanka and Durban, South Africa, remains involved in the business. She is Chair of the Board of Directors and administers international marketing and shipping business between the Americas, Asia, and Indonesia.

Home remains in Long Beach, California. Not the iconic Villa Riveria, where Rowland spent his formative years, and helped attend to his two younger sisters, Sophia and Isabella, but on Ocean Boulevard, in a classic home built in 1910. The house is three-storied with a commanding view of the beach, Pacific Ocean, and quite often, Catalina Island. And more recent, the ship Queen Mary, permentally based across the inlet from Long Beach Marina where the family sailing yacht, *Fair Wind*, is berthed.

Since old enough to write, which for Rowland, was at four years of age, he and Azra became pen-pals. Azra is a daughter of Eka and Adelia and lives in, Maputo, Mozambique, Africa. Eka and Adelia had long been close friends of Rowland's parents and are successful owners of a large fishing fleet and three canneries located along the coast of Mozambique with another situated on the coast of Durban, South Africa.

The calendar had said adieu to a troubled 70s decade. Jumping into the 1980s meant technology was the new game in countries and societies around the world. Computer companies and computer programmers were bent on driving commerce, and cultures, in fields of business and industry, education, science, politics, the military, and even the home. Rowland saw himself as being part of it and possessed the intellectual capacity to become a major player.

From Mozambique, word came that Azra was doing well in her studies at Oxford University. She had tracked her mother, Adelia, a great-granddaughter of Gungunhana, *The Lion of Gaza*, the last great King of an Empire covering Eastern Africa. Adelia had completed graduate studies in international business and economics at Oxford in the early 1960s and worked alongside her husband, Eka, in the fishing and fish canning industry.

But as 1983 begins, all is not well in Long Beach, Jakarta, or Mozambique. With prosperity comes jealousy and greed. With greed comes scheming men, and women serving the ambitions of nations. With scheming comes evil's darkness, manifest in threats, torture, and deadly force, where human beings take lives in cold blood. And, with evil hearts and malicious intent, destroy freedom.

Both families keep their strong friendship floating across far distances with assurance such a treasure will forever be preserved. But there are those in other parts of a shrinking world seeking to exploit devious opportunities that shake each family, and their enterprises, to the core. They do so with a history of no qualms about destroying competition and attacking by insidious means. Those who take that which is preciously guarded and revered by most, freedom, prosperity, and peace; those who descend like a foul, suffocating blanket on life!

Embedded within the families, are young, intelligent, and dedicated spirits. A young white man and young black woman, who eventually become husband and wife, who, even half a world apart, find ways to combat deadly threats. Azra, a tall, beautiful, intelligent, witty woman, places university life on hold, joining Rowland, an American of Dutch heritage. Together, they plunge headlong into the fray. As conditions go on, as challenges slither as snakes out of darkness, again and again, Azra becomes the *Lioness of Gaza*.

PROLOGUE

Do you see them? Where are they? They were supposed to carry a flag!"

"Patience grasshopper. They'll be at the boarding exit soon." Elsje responded.

"But Elsje, they're just kids! Just look at this mob of travelers!"

"I know Trace. But they have identification tags. Besides, they are in first class and have 'D,' and a flight attendant assigned to take special care of them. They'll likely be last to come off the plane."

"Well, why doesn't anyone let a guy know what's going on!" I responded. Adding, "What about this 'D', doesn't she have a real name?

Elsje groaned, saying. "Her name is Dorcus. But, please, do not call her that. She is seriously particular about referring to her only as 'D'. And, dear husband, she is about the best bodyguard anyone could hope for."

"I know, I know, she was with Mossad in Israel until something happened on some assignment in South Africa!" I whispered.

Elsje glanced at me and responded, "There are some things we just do not talk about!" Elsje then tossed one of her *"she who must be obeyed"* looks. I clammed up and focused on the exit door, watching for our grandchildren who had flown all the way from Maputo, Mozambique. *"Good grief!"* I thought, *"They must be absolutely exhausted!"*

Just then Elsje whispered, "There's 'D'!

"Where?" I asked.

"Just at the door, the short woman, in kaki bellbottoms and white tunic, the one with dark hair in a bun, sunglasses tipped back on her head," Elsje whispered.

I watched as 'D' paused, looked around, then spotted us and nodded. No smile. Following her was an American flag, waving, followed by a Dutch flag, bobbing. Held by our beautiful grandchildren, Terresa, the oldest at thirteen, and Tommy, who had his ninth birthday a month ago.

Close behind was a lovely, quite mature, American Airlines flight attendant holding documents. The instant the kids saw us, they screamed, "Papa, grandmama!" and ran to our open arms. 'D' kept lockstep in every stride they took.

"Are you Mr. Tracey Schaffer, and are you, madam, Mrs. Elsje Schaffer?" The flight attendant asked.

"Who else would we be?" I answered, with a smile, while hugging Tommy.

Elsje nudged me saying, "We are! And I suppose you have documents for us to sign?" The attendant responded, "Yes, I do." Then added, "Would you please provide some identification sir, and you as well, madam?"

As we showed the attendant our identification I noticed 'D', standing close to the stewardess, was also taking a look. She glanced at me twice. Still no smile. My California driver's license was nearly expired and the picture on it was a shade out of date. But my fresh US passport was handy, just in case.

Finally, after signing for the release of our grandchildren from American Airlines into our care, 'D' extended her hand, saying, "Mr. Schaffer, it is a pleasure to meet you. I have heard so much about you and Mrs. Schaffer." Her grip was firm, the shake brief. But, she then smiled, with a most disarming smile. With glitter in her lovely hazel eyes, she leaned forward and whispered, "Your grandkids are full of vinegar!" I whispered back, "They come by it naturally!"

After collecting luggage and having a steward assemble the pile of suitcases on a large cart, we were in the limo hired for the occasion, and on our way from a very busy LAX to Long Beach. The kids were gawking at the freeway and millions of cars traveling bumper to bumper at 80 miles an hour. Tommy, his nose pressed to the side window kept saying, "WOW!" and "Holy Cow papa! Too many cars!" I agreed!

Terresa tugged at Elsje's coat sleeve, and asked, "Grandmama, when do we go to Disneyland?" Elsje looked at me, smiled, and said, "Okay, I owe you a milkshake!"

"D' chuckled and asked, "What was the wager?"

"The first thing these kids would ask would be Disneyland! That's what I bet they would do." Then I looked back at Elsje, saying, "A giant strawberry shake would do nice!" We laughed.

Elsje hugged Teressa saying, "I'm thinking a couple of days after you have rested from your long journey." "Oh, but we are not tired! Are we Thomas?!" Terresa quickly responded. Tommy pulled away from the window muttering, "No, but I'm hungry!" "Thomas!" Terresa chided, "You know what I told you about *It's a Small World*!" "I know, but I'm hungry!" Tommy repeated. Terresa smiled, saying, "Thomas can be a pest."

It was clear Tommy's big sister was in charge. Terresa, for her part, speaking in perfect British English, did her best to appear all grown up. Yet, she had a charm about her that reflected the witty nature of her mother, Azara, and the stature of our son, her father, Rowland. Elsje looked at me, her countenance covered with motherly pride.

After slowing down, then doing the stop-and-go routine for a wreck between cars and a motorcyclist, lots of them on their Harleys or Hondas raced between lanes, we finally made it home.

Consuelo, our cook, Priscilla, our housemaid, a young black woman we helped escape a horribly abusive husband, along with Roy Oshida, a Japanese gardener who comes twice a week, all joined in lugging suitcases into the house and upstairs bedrooms. 'D' insisted on a bedroom next to the kids, quietly saying, "It's my job!"

After a light lunch and settling down in the study, the kids went to explore the backyard and help Roy with his landscape work, I asked 'D' about Rowland and Azra, and the situation in Mozambique. Elsje interrupted, asking, "First, how is Adelia doing?"

"Adelia is doing quite well. Her health is strong and she is very well looked after by a live-in woman companion and her bodyguards." Then 'D' added, "She offers her love and best wishes to you both." 'D' paused, shook her head a little, and added, "She misses her Eka so terribly that, at times, when at the main cannery at Maputo, she sits in her office, reading newspapers and waiting, as if, at any moment, Eka will walk through the door."

Elsje softly said, "Oh that breaks my heart. Poor Adelia."

'D' quickly responded, "Oh she is quite happy and busy…really! When she comes to the office she tells the most fantastic tales about temples on Sumatra Island, diamonds, emeralds, and gold!" Adding, "She even flashes a couple of incredible rings she claims were once worn by an ancient Sumatran princes."

I glanced at Elsje and she at me. We just smiled.

Then 'D' asked a question. "If you don't mind, Mr. Schaffer, and feel it appropriate, I would appreciate a better understanding of what happened at Jakarta and Durban back in 1980 and 81'. I was brought on board to oversee security for the family by your son shortly after, but Rowland is pretty mum about what occurred and how Eka, who was apparently so well respected and loved, was killed.

I glanced at Elsje. She nodded. Then I said, "Tell you what, 'D', after Disneyland, how would you like to go for a sail to Catalina Island and spend a few days relaxing at Cherry Cove and Avalon Harbor?" 'D' became wide-eyed and responded, "I'd love it!"

At that moment, the phone rang. Priscilla took the call, came into the study, and whispered to Elsje. "Elsje jumped up and glanced at me, saying, "It's Azra! Go get the kids, she will want to talk with them!"

Priscilla, held up her hand toward me saying, "No worries sir, I'll get the kids." Then she darted for the back door leading to the gardens. 'D' got up and followed Priscilla. I picked up the receiver in my office to listen in. Both Rowland and Azra were on the line, laughing and talking with Elsje about the Disneyland wager. As soon as I had a chance I butted in, letting them know how proud we are of their parenting. Azra, in her own excellent British English, said, "Keeping up with those two is a challenge. Hope they do not wear you down before we arrive."

Elsje chimed in asking, "Have your flight arrangements and visas been confirmed? Rowland responded, "Had a little trouble with the American side of the fence but got things straightened out!" Azra added, "They are no worse than the British"! Elsje then said, "We had a chat with 'D' and she says your mom is doing well." Yes, very well! We keep her busy which seems to help." "Please give her my love," Elsje responded.

I took up the subject we had just discussed with 'D' asking, "Do you have any problems our sharing with 'D' about Eka and the Van Steenwijk Inter-Island Shipping battle with the Russian mafia?" There was a momentary pause. Then Rowland said, "Dad, just be certain she knows there are some matters that must remain confidential." "I know son, I know."

Azra spoke, saying, "'D' is well vetted and knows the rules. I, we, trust her completely. And as for my dad, well, there remains some unsolved matters which are yet to be discovered." "I know Azra," I responded. Adding, "Who knows, maybe she can help."

"Dad, perhaps it would be well for me to discuss matters related to Eka when we are there with you." I responded, "Son, let's leave it be as you wish. I will tell the rest of the story." Elsje quickly commented, "And, I shall make sure he tells it as it actually happened!" "Thanks, Mom!" Rowland responded. They laughed.

So, the kids are fine! 'D' is attending! Disneyland is first on the to-do list, and then sailing to Catalina! And you will arrive in about two weeks!" I summarized. Elsje jumped in, saying, "And we have a new cell phone, and the satellite phone is on the boat, you know the number. So, if you need, call any time!" Elsje added, "And, son, please call your sister! Sophia is busy with the company in Jakarta but says she needs to talk and has not had a response from you.

"Will do Mom! It's been a little dicey here in Maputo, new government and all, you know. No excuse, but Sophia is on my call list." Rowland then inquired, "How's Isabella doing in her master's program at MIT?" "Just fine!" Elsje and I responded together. Then I added, "She will finish this next spring and was interviewed two weeks ago for a position at White Sands! No details." "All hush-hush stuff!" Elsje added.

The kids came running in. The conversation was totally turned over to them as they energetically competed for talk time with their mom and dad. Terresa told about the layover at Atlanta, Georgia, and how gracious American Airlines Admiral Club people were for their six-hour stay. Tommy jabbered about the Los Angeles freeways, and Roy, the Japanese gardener, made them laugh with his bowing and strange talk.

Elsje and I had finished our talking, and bade adieus when Rowland asked for 'D'. I put her on the line and went outside with the kids, at their insistence, so they could show me the bougainvillea climbing over a high wall. And, hummingbirds busy sucking nectar at several feeders.

The Mexican dinner, so very well prepared by Consuelo, was the sleeping pill the kids needed to mellow their invincible energy. And, carefully observing 'D', she as well would benefit from a good sound sleep.

An hour later, the house was quiet. Elsje and I sat in lounge chairs on the back deck, where Priscilla had lit tiki lanterns, sipping warm tea. We rehearsed the story I was about to share with 'D'. I was quickly being corrected on a few points. Elsje, with a smile, commented "You know, grasshopper, you really are broad brush!"

I responded, "I suppose. And you, sweet lady, are detail. And that makes it work!"

Elsje then commented, "Those were terrible days for the Van Steenwijk's and a host of others." Then she shifted, looked at me, and added, "You know, perhaps 'D' can help tie some loose ends together. I understand she still has strong ties with Mossad." She paused, then quietly said, "Perhaps…even perhaps, we can discover who killed Eka."

"Sweetheart, that all began when the 80s came into view. It's been, what, near seven years!" I muttered.

"I know. But there are lingering dangers which could affect Rowland and Azra, and Adelia…and us! You know as well as I they dealt those Russians a defeat, totally!" Elsje was a little animated. I reached out, took her hand, gently squeezed, then whispered, "We shall see, we shall see."

1

Jakarta

Disneyland was an absolute hoot for the kids, and for 'D'. We spent the whole day and stayed for the fireworks. Terresa and Tommy had pictures taken with Mickey Mouse and Snow White, along with a couple of elves. The next day Elsje took the kids, with 'D', staying close, shopping for the sail to Catalina.

They took a drive through Naples Island. The kids were surprised to see Zietan's, a true mom-and-pop store, meet Bob Zietan, and order meat from the butcher shop. Elsje then took them to see where Rowland, the German, had lived. Then on to more shopping, including Trader Joe's! "They let me ring the ship's bell!" Tommy excitedly told me later.

Our sail to Cherry Cove, where a rock outcropping on the west side is the shape of a Lion's Head, was a slow and gentle crossing. Fair Wind performed perfectly and both Terresa and Tommy were thrilled to take the helm, steering the yacht to an island, a new and strange place, for them. And, watch dolphins jump and play in a blue-green sea.

After picking up a mooring can, they were all the more delighted in watching beautiful golden Garibaldi fish swimming all about the cove in crystal clear water.

During the crossing, I began telling the story. 'D' intently listened. Elsje was just as intently, it seemed, ready to offer corrections.

"It was early 1983, February I believe. Elsje was in Jakarta, handling a ton of company matters, when I received a strange call at my office here in Long Beach. The call came from a VP with one of my clients, The Irvine Company, of Newport Beach, telling me they had received an inquiry about my dealings with a certain New York long shoreman union boss and shipping company in Indonesia, the Van Steenwijk Inter-Island Shipping Company. When I asked who was making the inquiries, all they knew was he had called from somewhere in the Turkman region of the USSR. He identified himself as "Dima", with no surname. And, no information was given by the Irvine Company."

"Turkman was a dangerous area and still is! 'D' commented.

"Well, a few days later, I received a call from a woman who said her name was "Kira", that she represented a Soviet law firm making inquiries for a client, she would not disclose who, with an interest in purchasing the Van Steenwijk business in Jakarta."

"She called you twice dear and the main office in Jakarta at least three times!" Elsje added.

"Yes! Right!" I responded. Adding, "At first it all seemed like some nuisance stuff, you know, like robocalls, marketing idiots, that kind of nonsense. So, business as usual. Right?"

"Did you give them any contact information or company information, anything they may have been asking for?" 'D' asked.

"No, nothing!" Elsje responded. I added, "Nada!"

"It was nearly three months later, just after Elsje returned from Jakarta, that we received a call from the Durban office." "Early, about 2:30 in the morning!" Elsje added.

"That's right!" I confirmed. "There was trouble on the docks. Several men, who were not locals, nor had been seen before, were seen messing with sealed containers. They had opened four, were spraying something inside, then ran to a waiting black van that burned rubber getting away. But two company workers confirmed the license plate and after Durban police checked, discovered the vehicle was rented."

"Who too?" 'D' asked.

"They paid cash and the names registered on the rental agreement were convoluted, they were miss-spelled Dutch names that were far from common. Old, very old Dutch names." I responded.

"What did they spray into the containers?" 'D' inquired. "It was canisters, actually, like about the size of propane tanks used for camp stoves," Elsje commented. "Yes, that's right, like camp stove canisters for propane. But was not propane!" I added. Then Elsje said, "Lab reports identified it as a chemical compound called Lewisite/Mustard!" Adding, "The SSA, South Africa Security Agency, in cooperation with Interpol agents, confirmed the stuff was created by the Soviet military somewhere near Gorny, Russia."

'Yes! But many terrorist factions have access to that stuff. It's lethal!" 'D' grimly stated. Then asked, "Were any of your people hurt?" "Not too bad. One was hospitalized for about a month. He was warned not to open the container and look but disregarded the warning." Elsje responded.

"Lucky he didn't die!" 'D' firmly commented. Elsje and I looked at each other, recalling that the fellow was not able to return to work, likely for the rest of his life!

"Yes, well!" I continued, "It was an event that certainly got our attention. There was an investigation but nothing could be confirmed except we were dealing with some type of organized gang or group! Two agents agreed, from security camera video of the bad guys, after they removed gasmasks that we may be dealing with eastern Europeans and or Middle Eastern thugs, for there was an ethnic mix of men included in the imagery taken."

"Some of the gas escaped and people up and down the dock, so we were told, felt the effects but it was slight," I added. Elsje looked at me and whispered, "Not so slight for some."

'D' gave us a serious look, then said, "You had a shot across your corporate bow! And it may well have been the heavy artillery, meaning state-sponsored!"

"You are dead right on that score 'D'," Elsje responded. "Yes! By all we were able to discover, with help from our son, Rowland, and his wife, Azra, we have a strong notion what happened was more than gang stuff. And, later, as the situation worsened, it became clear". I added.

What was it that convinced you?" 'D' asked.

"I shall relate that part of the story after I barbeque some steaks for dinner," I responded. 'D' Smiled. Elsje hollered for the kids. I pulled out the barbeque stuff.

Then, 'D''s attention turned to Terresa and Tommy rowing the dingy around the cove, chatting with other couples and kids on the many fine yachts now tethered to mooring cans at Cherry Cove. She asked if we had binoculars. I handed them to her and watched as she focused on the kids, and other yachts, saying, "Don't normally let them get this far away in public!"

Elsje casually commented, "I'm pretty sure they are in good company here." 'D' glanced at Elsje, then me, saying, it has become a dangerous world. Folks of your financial status, more particularly, are a juicy target."

Her comment brought an instant recall of the Red Turbans in Sumatra and Sri Lanka. Though different circumstances, what surfaced in those thoughts was Elsje pleading that the thing end. I wondered if we were, actually, finished with the Russians and their henchmen. As I turned, I caught Elsje looking at me. In her eyes, I saw the same question. Daily life has a way of cloaking unwanted realities.

Looking at 'D', as she returned to slowly scanning boats moored in the cove, there was no doubt. The fact she was there at all, doing what she was charged to do, settled the matter. What had Rowland and Azra not told us? I wondered.

A few moments later, Terresa and Tommy bumped the dinghy into the side of the boat. Tommy was rowing. Terresa was giving Tommy heck, saying, "I told you not to row so fast!" Tommy stuck his tongue out. To which Terresa said,

"Children, so disgusting!" With the help of 'D,' they were aboard and clamoring for the head to wash up. Elsje shouted down below, "Be kind and take your time, dinner will be ready in about an hour." 'D' smiled and whispered, "Full of vinegar!"

Dinner in a cove aboard Fair Wind was always memorable. The weather was so pleasant there was every reason to have a little dessert. Some delicious Polenta, with hot chocolate, was enjoyed in the cockpit. During a lull in the conversation, a nanny-goat called for her kids, somewhere up on the island. Some Boy Scout leaders were having a campfire meeting on the beach. Preparing, no doubt, for the arrival of a few troops for a campout and to work on merit badges. Just as light began to fade and Elsje was readying the anchor lantern, a flock of pelicans gracefully flew by.

"Well, where was I?" I asked. Elsje responded, "Cannisters thrown into the containers at the Durban docks!"

"Right, Right." I said and was about to say more when Terresa quietly interrupted, "Ivankov!" Her face was dower, her lips drawn tight, her eyes dead-pan and steadied directly at me, then she turned her gaze toward Elsje.

'D' leaned forward and asked, "What did you say?" Terresa looked at 'D' with that same steady gaze and repeated, "Ivankov!" 'D' looked at me, then Elsje, and quietly asked us, "Have you heard that name before?" Both of us, looking at Terresa, slowly shook our heads no. Then 'D' asked Terresa, "Where did you hear that name?" Terresa hesitated, then looking 'D' straight in the eye, said, "I overheard Mom and Dad talking. They were talking about the attacks on the

Van Steenwijk's ships and warehouses, and Dad said they had new information that Ivankov who works for Bratva was the leader!"

Terresa sat motionless yet poised, full of resolve and purpose. So much so, in that moment, she reminded me of Eka dispatching cobras at the Sumatran Temple. I ventured a question, asking, what else did your folks say about this Ivankov and Bratva?" "Only that someday, somehow, there would be justice for such evil." Terresa firmly responded.

"Justice for whom?" Elsje asked.

"Justice for Ivankov, his men, the whole Bratva mob!" Terresa sternly replied.

"It is the Solntsevskaya Bratva, a Russian mafia mob with strong connections to politicians, financial institutions, and military organizations throughout the globe!" 'D' quietly said. Then she added, "They are active here in your country. Well established and have been for decades."

Elsje motioned Terresa to come and sit close to her. Then she wrapped her arms around Terresa and kissed her gently on the forehead. We were all silent for a short spell. When I suggested the children be readied for bed, Terresa resisted, saying, "I know a lot, but Mom and Dad asked me not to talk of it. But if you are…well then…" Elsje interrupted, saying, "Sweetheart, if you want to stay up a while that will be fine." Elsje looked over at me as she continued, saying, "I am confident Papa will not be talking of things you don't already know or have heard."

I looked over toward Tommy discovering he was asleep on a cushion in the corner of the cockpit. Picking him up, I looked down at Terresa and whispered, "You wore your brother out with all that rowing today!" She smiled. I smiled back and carried the tike down to his berth.

When I returned, 'D' was asking Terresa questions. Terresa seemed confident, exhibiting the importance of being accurate in what she said, and obviously well-schooled in retaining integrity in all she said. I was amazed when she revealed she was seven years old when she first heard the name, Ivankov. 'D' responded, relating that the full name of the man is Viktor Ivankov. Terresa thought a moment, then said, 'That is true. Yes, that is his complete Russian name."

Elsje suggested I relate what else we knew of the affair. I sipped my hot chocolate, now "lukewarm" chocolate, and began.

Looking at Elsje for confirmation, I said, "The initial damages, products destroyed in the four containers, was over a million dollars, US." Elsje shook her head, adding, $1,346,244 US." Then smiled, saying, "Yes. Well, that was, as you say, 'D', the first shot fired across the bow."

Elsje continued, "Three months later the Morning Star, one of the finest ships the Van Steenwijk's own, mysteriously developed serious engine problems and sat dead in the water, at anchor, off the Port of Jakarta for a month. The perishables aboard quickly spoiled leaving a horrific smell, carried by breezes into the city. It became so bad that the ship was towed far out into the sea, and the entire load dumped overboard. That was another three-million-dollar loss. An investigation found that fine, nearly microscopic, metal shavings had been put in the ship's fuel system."

Then I said, "Then, not more than two months later, the crew of the Northern Star, another fine Van Steenwijk vessel, became deathly sick, with ten dying of some virus, a compound of unknown origin. Some analysts suspected the Ukraine state of the USSR. That affair cost the company over five million dollars, US." Elsje injected. Saying, $5.2!"

I added, "So, in less than six months, there had been three major incidents costing lives and losses of nearly 10 million dollars, US." Elsje again injected, saying, $9,687,520, US.

"You were under attack!" 'D' muttered, shaking her head. "Yes!" Elsje exclaimed, "We were being attacked and at first, the several governments we were dealing with, would only politely listen!" "Except!" I inserted, "The CIA and Dutch Intelligence Services." I continued, "But even they, at first, gave the Van Steenwijk's difficulties minimal interest. And, that's when our son Rowland and his wife Azra became aware of what was going on and determined to engage."

'D' leaned forward saying, "My time with Mossad was far shorter than I'd hoped for. I would be with them now except I went through a breakdown of sorts when my fiancé, a team partner with special operations, was beheaded by Arabs in Jordan. I was there, forced to watch then molested and later rescued." 'D' paused a moment. Then added, "On that particular mission, we were trying to catch and dispatch members of a Russian mob who had ties with Bratva and the Islamic Brotherhood. A key player was Viktor Ivankov!"

Terresa spoke quietly, sadly, saying, "There were Arabs with the men who killed my Oupa, Eka. My mom saw them when they captured Oupa and took him away somewhere."

Terresa cupped her hands to her face and cried. Elsje cuddled Terresa close, patted her head, and then whispered, "Someday we just might find those men and bring them to justice."

Elsje looked at 'D' asking, "Are you able to pick up on Ivankov's trail?"

'D' shook her head, saying, "Doubtful?"

"Does that mean there is a possibility or no way Jose?" I asked.

'D' looked at us a moment, gave a wry smile, then leaned back against the gunnel and said, "It may stir a hornet's nest, and no promises, you understand, but I'll make an inquiry when we get back to Long Beach. There are some friends with Mossad who, I know, would love to have a shot at getting Ivankov!"

Elsje and I glanced at each other and nodded in agreement. Agreeing the matter be dealt with. A moment later I continued the story, as best I knew of it, saying, "Right after the third incident, about a week or ten days, the Jakarta office had a visit from three men. They had heavy Russian accents but spoke English quite well. The lead man introduced himself as Alexi Lebedev, the other two were Lev and Dima, the same, we thought, as the guy making phone calls. They wanted to arrange a meeting with the owners to discuss the purchase of the company."

"Purchase by who?" 'D' asked. "They said they represented The Estonia Shipping Company of Tallinn, Estonia," Elsje responded, adding, "They presented documents and identification which had the USSR stamp plastered all over their papers."

"Easily counterfeited!" 'D' quipped. Then asked, "Did you grant the meeting?"

"No!" Elsje responded. "The executive we hired to run operations in Jakarta told the men, "You fellows must have the wrong shipping company, or be lost, the Van Steenwijk Inter-Island Company is not for sale!"

"How did they respond? 'D' inquired.

"From what we learned, they were furious, complaining they had traveled so far for nothing. Then the leader, Alexi, said a curious thing; he said, "There may come a day soon when you will have wished to sell while the company still had value!". Then they left in a huff!" Elsje said. I interjected, saying, "We, Dutch Security Services, actually, tried their best to locate the three Russians but could not find a trace. They were nowhere in Jakarta or that region. It was as if they were ghosts."

"Anyway," I continued, "About a month later, it was late October of 1983, The Perseverance was returning from Australia to Jakarta with a load of cargo and was near Port Moresby when a distress call went out that the ship had been attacked and was being taken over by pirates! What happened was that the pirates who boarded Perseverance murdered the captain and all the crew, except one, the chief engineer, who apparently had not been discovered, and sailed it, we know from what satellite imagery we had at first, in an easterly direction. Then the transponders were shut down."

"Sometime later, a brief emergency call was picked up by US military intelligence in Alaska. It was made by the engineer. The transponders had been turned back on and the ship Perseverance had entered Peter the Great Bay off The Sea Of Japan. It was headed for Vladivostok. After that, Perseverance simply disappeared! The engineer was never heard from again." Adding, "We believe he was killed after being discovered!"

Elsje added, "That was a huge blow to the company financially. But the greater blow was the loss of our captain and crew. Altogether, 31 men and five women were dead!"

That is when Dutch Security Services and Interpol began to take a stronger interest." I said. "But you know, it was all too late, too little and too shallow an effort. And, the company was facing some very hard times!"

"Just where jackals want to herd you before the kill! 'D' quietly commented.

I looked at Elsje and saw that Terresa had fallen asleep. Motioning to Elsje, She lifted Terresa a little, saying, "Bedtime sweetheart." The two went down into the cabin where Terresa was soon in the sack.

While they were gone, I said to 'D', "You know, that horrible smell in Jakarta, from the first incident, should have triggered our organizing a defense. We failed in that regard. It's something I regret. This whole affair has wreaked havoc on my Elsje, her company, and on hundreds of lives!" 'D' shook her head saying, "Oh, those marvelous and confounding words, *should have*!"

After Elsje returned we talked for an hour or so. Before retiring, 'D' suggested it may be well to think carefully about building that defense we failed to fully consider nearly ten years before. "For", she flatly said, "I'm anxious to hear what Rowland and Azra have to add. But I must say, here and now, from all I am gathering, and what I know of firsthand, you may not be through with the Russians and their hired thugs, the Bratva, and perhaps, even, Ivankov!"

Elsje embraced 'D' saying, "So thankful you are looking after our family. So grateful you are here." 'D' got wide-eyed. She was a little taken aback by the show of affection. I smiled, and said, "Don't worry, it's just the spirit of sailing and Catalina!" We chuckled and soon after retired.

Later I whispered to Elsje, "Did I get the story straight?" Her response was, "Close!" I pounded the pillow and snuggled down, listened to wavelets lapping at the hull, and fell into a deep, restful sleep, far and away from Russian thugs.

2

A Long Reach

W hat is that racket!" I shouted.

"The Boy Scouts have invaded Cherry Cove!" Elsje responded. She added, "About time you woke up. Breakfast is almost ready and the kids are with 'D' in the cockpit watching the show."

"What show?" I asked as I fumbled my way to the head.

Seems more than a few First Class, Second Class and Tenderfoot Scouts are doing their best to row canoes as close to Fair Wind as possible just to say hello to Terresa!" Elsje responded.

"Well, at least they can stop bumping into our boat!" I shouted while gargling. Then added, "Like a school of crazed sharks!"

"Right, you are, grasshopper! Right, you are" Elsje laughed and went up the ladder into the cockpit shouting, "At ease boys! It's time for our breakfast!"

A collective groan, followed by a few more bumps, from energized scouts and I was about to charge up the passageway, present myself as Captain Bligh, and say a word or two. Elsje motioned me back, pointing at the table holding a feast suitable for an Admiral. In a flash, Tommy was down, followed in close step by Terresa, then 'D' who was waving goodbye to a bunch of very demoralized Scouts.

"Wonder what merit badge they're working on?" I muttered.

"Now, now!" Elsje whispered.

That afternoon we sailed for Moonstone Cove. I knew the caretaker who delighted in tossing freshly caught lobsters into the cockpit. We did not complain! 'D' was absolutely delighted, as were the kids. That evening was so very special as a delicious lobster dinner was capped by a crimson sky that settled over Catalina, reminding us of that old saying, "Red sky at night, sailors delight!"

It had been a busy day. However, 'D' insisted we continue the Jakarta account. Terresa and Tommy had been swimming after dinner and returned to the boat a little cold, and more than a little tired. After warm showers, they were ready for the sack. Elsje and I had a rare grandparent pleasure of tucking them in their berths, reciting silly stories about the way the world was when we were kids. They did not last long. I'd barely begun when both were drifting with the gentle rocking motion of Fair Wind, secure on a mooring at Moonstone.

"Some hot chocolate anyone?" Elsje asked.

"Absolutely!" Both 'D' and I responded. The evening air had turned a bit chilly.

After we were settled in the cockpit with Nautica lap throws, Elsje re-started the story, saying, "Well, it was sometime after the loss of Perseverance and her crew that we began to receive helpful intelligence from our friends in

Dutch Security Services. We were told that according to two informants, the Russians were determined to establish themselves as masters of illegal drug transporters throughout Indonesia, India, and Africa. And to do that they needed a legitimate shipping company they could control and manipulate. Ours, it seemed, was their favored company, the Van Steenwijk Inter-Island Shipping!"

I interjected, "If they could not acquire the company, they would bring it to bankruptcy and then claim it for pennies on the dollar value!"

Elsje continued, "So, what we began to realize, was that all the little and not-so-little issues which affected the business, mounting up to huge financial losses, were orchestrated by the Russian government through the Russian mafia operating out of Turkman and were led by Ivankov." Elsje paused, took a long sip of hot chocolate, and then, looking at 'D', said, "And that's when we realized we were actually under attack. An emergency board meeting was held with Interpol and Dutch Security present."

"What came out of the meeting?" 'D' asked.

"Absolutely nothing of worth! Absolutely nothing!" Elsje responded. Then added, "We were feeling pretty demoralized at the time and after some discussion, we decided to have a conference call with the kids, that is Rowland, and his bride Azra, whom he was engaged to marry after graduating from university studies, that they may be aware of the dangers we were facing."

I added, "It was shortly after that call, a long and difficult call, that we had a call from Eka in Mozambique. Azra had informed her father of our situation. He then revealed that his fishing company was experiencing some of the same troubles. That is when Eka and Adelia, Elsje and I, and the kids, Rowland and Azra, decided we needed a plan. A defense. A way to stop the Russians cold, even if it meant using lethal means!"

'D' took a long sip and remained quiet for a moment. Then leaned back and wistfully said, "So, that's why all the security needed for the business, the family, and for Eka and Adelia! I wondered why there was such a strong need for security. Thought it was because of the Mozambique civil war, the bloodletting between Frelima and the Rnamo, and several other factions!" Then, looking at us, she added, "You realized, of course, the dangerous situation you were in!" 'D' paused, then asked, "So, what was the plan, and how did you carry it out?"

"Well..." I started to say. But Elsje interrupted saying, "Trace, we promised Rowland and Azra that they would share the details when they arrive."

"Right!" I responded, shaking my head in agreement. Then, smiling at 'D', I said, "All I can say is, while we think we have all the answers, as adults and parents, I mean, it is amazing how resourceful and capable the younger generation can be, especially in this new computer, internet, and digital age!" Elsje added, "Particularly when they make up their mind to do a thing! Well, when they do, stand back! They get the bit in their teeth and make an amazing run of it!"

'D' smiled. Then said, "Obviously you made progress in what was happening, what, some seven or eight years ago?

"Question is, are the Russians through with you, and Rowland and Azara, and Adelia, and The Van Steenwijk Shipping Company? Or, are they plotting another approach?" She sipped her hot chocolate, then added, "If I measure this correctly, and draw on what I know, or knew when I left Mossad, the Russians are tenacious! They too, can get the 'bit in their teeth'! And, believe me, will run over anyone who gets their way!"

"We know." Elsje quietly said. The loss of Eka, and the way he died, was nearly more than we could bear."

I thought for a moment, back to what happened and felt it safe, and not intrusive on what Rowland would be relating, then said, "As Elsje just said, we know, or at least we have had an unhealthy dose of Russian tactics and their aggression. At the time, when fear was slipping into despair, we reached for help in several directions. There was little offered. And when we called Azra and Rowland to let them know what was going on, it became a family affair for survival."

Elsje interrupted, saying, "At first we were dismissive, doubtful, and certainly cautious when the kids said, they wanted to help in the fight. I did not want them exposed to such dangers, or, disrupt their university studies. I resisted the idea out of hand. But, two weeks later, they both showed up at our home, unannounced and said, "We have a plan!" I interjected, "And that, 'D', is what Rowland and Azra will explain, along with how they, we that is, did it with the help of Dutch Security and others."

It was late. We turned in and found the night to be quiet and restful. The next day we went ashore and took a long hike on island trails, climbing up above the cove. Looking down, we could see the translucent blue water. Fair Wind sat beautifully casting a shadow on the sandy bottom. We could hear, barely, the small bronze bell, we called 'tinker-bell' ringing delicately in a westerly breeze.

Three days passed, and far too quickly, at Moonstone Cove. We sailed to Avalon Harbor where we stayed a few more days, hiking around the village, combing through shops, and totally enjoying a Silent Film Festival at the Casino. The kids, even 'D', were blown away by Charlie Chapman, Lillian Gish, Buster Keaton, Colleen Moore, Anita Stewart, and others of that incredible film era full of good against evil plots, boos and hisses, intrigue, and crazy stunts.

After lying on the beach, licking ice cream cones, savoring smoked barracuda, or gulping down corn dogs, which the kids preferred, we dined at my favorite Italian restaurant. Then, before sailing home, we paid a visit to the Marlin Club. It was a tradition to enter that historic place. A place that came to life in the late 1940s and hosted many of Hollywood's most famous celebrities. The kids loved it. We all did!

The sail home was fast. A westerly breeze was clocking about 20 knots and Fair Wind, while not the sailing craft as was Typee, made good headway. Dolphins joined the race as did a few sea birds. Within about four hours we were tied off at our slip in the Long Beach Marina. Terresa and Tommy pleaded to tour the Queen Mary. Elsje promised them that we would, "in a day or so". I'd seen it and pleaded for mercy, saying I needed to meet with a couple of clients. I actually did!

A few days passed. The kids climbed all over the Queen Mary. I reluctantly bowed to the occasion and joined them. Surprisingly, I saw some things and learned a few things missed before. When I asked the tour guide why they dumped all those wonderful teak deck lounging chairs overboard while out at sea, just before bringing the ship into Long Beach Harbor, she just smiled and shrugged her shoulders.

"It's Rowland dear!" Elsje announced. A few moments later she handed the phone to me, whispering, "They are in Dallas and decided it best to stay there a day or so as Azara is not feeling well."

"Hello, little grasshopper!" My salutation was well received as they both laughed, responding, "Hello back, big grasshopper!" "Where are you?" I asked. "We booked into the Adolphus here in Dallas. My sweetheart has a bad cold and needs to rest. Curious, we were delayed in Cairo by authorities, likely because of the situation in Mozambique, the fighting and all, which, by the way, looks to be about over!" Rowland responded.

"We are anxious to see you but take all the time you need." I said, "Dad, we will be there in a couple of days, Thursday or Friday!" Rowland responded. Azra then asked, "How are the kids?" "Having a blast! We've been sailing the last ten days and they have nearly worn Elsje and me out, but we're loving it!" I responded. Azara commented, "You know, papa, they are full of vinegar!" "Totally!" I shouted back.

"Dad, is 'D' available?" Rowland asked. "Yes, she's in the study, I'll put her on, just hang on a moment." I went to the study and told 'D' to pick up the phone, it was Rowland and Azara. They talked for several moments, and then she handed the phone back to me, saying, "Your son, sir."

"Yes, Rowland." "Dad, listen carefully. There have been some recent events that have us on guard." "What's happening?" I asked. "All I can say is we were followed from Cario to Madrid, and from there to Miami. The same man who was surveilling us, was on a cell phone while glancing at us, and while I'm not certain who he is, Azara and I agree, he's eastern European, could be Ukrainian!"

"Is he still following you?" I asked.

"Not certain Dad! The last we saw of him was at Miami International. But Azara says she thought she caught a glimpse of the same man at Dallas Airport when we got off. She said he was on the plane, sitting in the back, regular seating. Then she spotted him again near the terminal as we were getting into a taxi. As we left, I looked back, and sure enough, the same guy was on his cell."

"Do you have a good description?" I asked. Rowland chuckled, then said, "Better than that, big grasshopper, I have three photos of the creep! You know, the new camera technology set inside books. Spy stuff! I'm sending them to 'D' tonight." Then Rowland added, "Dad, you really need to get yourself one of the new laptop computers!"

"I know, I know! Your mom keeps saying the same!" I responded.

We talked a little longer. After goodbyes, I turned and looked at 'D', saying, "You may be right! It sounds like the Russians may have plans." 'D' looked straight at me and said,

"After I receive the images, I will be contacting my friends at Mossad and we shall, hopefully, discover who we are dealing with." Then she added, "If this is a known bad guy, my friends will know. Trust me, Mr. Schaffer, they will certainly know!"

Elsje came in carrying a worried look. She took my hand, saying, "Husband, please tell me we are not going to have troubles from the Russians...again?" 'D' excused herself, saying, "I need to check on the rug rats!" Her comment brought a chuckle from Elsje. Not quite certain what 'D' meant, I asked, "Rug rats?" Elsje laughed, saying, "Yes, grasshopper, your little grand-rug-rats! The ones full of vinegar!" I did not, could not, answer her question. My gut was protesting a possibility trouble was incubating!

Rowland and Azara arrived. It was Friday evening. An uncommon and quite unexpected rain, with lightning and rambunctious thunder, made unloading the limo a challenge. Ocean Boulevard was jammed with rush hour traffic. The kind of traffic testing nerves and dexterity when opening a street-side door. We left that task to the driver who kept decorum while other drivers honked.

Terresa and Tommy were totally excited, yammering every detail of their time sailing and while on Catalina Island. Including, seeing buffalo and wild goats, and eating corndogs on the beach at Avalon Harbor!

As soon as possible, Elsje had Azra in her arms asking if she was feeling better. Azra assured her that she was fine, saying, "It was a bit of virous. I had some meds handy that did the little devil in, quick-like!"

Rowland, looking a little worn, plopped on the living room couch. His first words, beyond hello, and we made it, were, "So good to be out of the rat race!" I sat down next to him, put an arm around him, and responded, welcome home son. Thankful you are safe!"

Elsje, the kids, and Azra went to the kitchen. 'D' stayed with Rowland and me. She took a seat near the couch. Rowland looked at her a moment, shook his head up and down, then quietly said, "I know what you are going to ask, and the answer is yes. But they changed the shadow to a girl, a tall, slender girl with red hair. We saw them, the guy and a new actor, together at Dallas, across the street from the hotel when we were loading to return to the airport. But the girl didn't board, at Dallas, and we did not see anything suspicious at LAX."

'D' quietly commented, "Well, I have some troubling information to share that I received this morning from Mossad. I was waiting for you and Azra to arrive and now that you are here, we should talk about it."

"I'll get Azra and Elsje. I offered. Rowland objected, saying, "Best they stay with the kids Dad. You and I can relate this to them later." "You're right son. Go ahead 'D', what do you have."

With a scowl, 'D' said, "According to a close friend in Tele Aviv, the man following you is *Sergi Lebedev*, a low-level hound dog with Bratva. However, he is also a close bodyguard for Ivankov, and wanted for murder, torture, and kidnapping in France, Belgium, and the UK." He is dangerous and skillful with the knife and razor belt he liberally uses to torture victims."

Looking at Rowland, 'D' continued, "I am sorry to add, that the girl you describe is very likely *Alina Volkov*. If it is her, she is quite dangerous. She wears wigs and has a unique ability to disguise herself in many different characters. But she has a tattoo on her right shoulder. It is a small image of the face of a wolf, same as the meaning of her surname in Russian. And," 'D' added, "She's the darling of *Solntsevskaya*, head of Bratva!"

"We have a problem!" I muttered. 'D' spoke quietly, saying, "We need to go into close protective mode, and that will require some discussion with your family, and certainly with your people in Jakarta, Mr. Shaffer, and your people in Maputo, Rowland."

I looked up to see Elsje standing at the opening of the living room. She was ringing a dishtowel and had the most sour look. Immediately, I went to her side and embraced her. She whispered, "What more evil can these people impose upon us?" Then, quite unlike her, she cursed. "Damn them to hell!" Then abruptly turned and went back toward the kitchen.

Rowland got up and went after his mother. I looked at 'D' who was staring at the floor. She too held a sour look. But, a moment later, 'D' turned toward me saying, "I think it's time to call in a few favors. May I use the satellite phone on your boat? I need to contact Mossad headquarters in Israel."

"By all means!" I responded. "I'll get the car. Gather what you need and meet me in the garage. We'll go by the alley."

'D' nodded and went upstairs to the bedroom floor. I had no doubt she was getting her weapon, a Beretta 92FS – 9mm with a 17-round mag.

I glanced out the window and confirmed the rain had all but stopped. Then went to the kitchen where Elsje, the kids, and Azra, were busy making cookies, all with Consuelo's close supervision. Then went to a back room closet and opened the vault where I kept weapons rescued from Typee off the coast of Madagascar. I selected the sawed-off 12 gauge.

Elsje came to me asking, "Are we going to war?" "Just in case," I responded. Then said, "'D' is going to use the satellite phone to call her people in Israel. Be certain the doors are kept locked. We will be back soon." Rowland poked his head in and asked, "Dad, where are the rest of the weapons and ammo?" I pointed to the vault and said, "Take your pick, son."

'D' came to the door and nodded she was ready. I kissed Elsje, looked at my son with pride and assurance he, and Azra, could handle themselves well, as could Elsje, and turned to 'D' saying, "Let's went!" She hesitated, gave me a curious look, and was about to ask, when I smiled saying, "It's what Poncho says to Cisco when they need to go!" 'D' shook her head and muttered, "Hollywood, home of the Wild West!"

After checking to see if we were followed, we walked down the marina dock and opened up Fair Wind. Once below, 'D' took the satellite phone and began the protocols needed to connect. After some code language, she began a conversation in Hebrew. In all, she spent half an hour in what, at times, was a rather energized conversation. I had gone topside and looked around. Hardly anyone was about except a couple of linemen working on replacing streetlamps. Then 'D' called me to the phone.

"Yes, this is Tracy Schaffer!" The man talking, who spoke distinct English, simply said, "We are going to assist you in this matter. Are you willing to have your life turned upside down?" I took a breath and then said, "If it saves family, friends, and our business, then yes. I am willing and do all I can to help!" His response was, "Good! We will be in touch! And, by the way, 'D' loves Babka!" Then laughed and hung up.

I gave a curious look at 'D', asking, "Babka?" She actually blushed and laughed at the same time. "So, where do we find Babka?" I asked. "Anywhere you find healthy Jews!" 'D' responded. Then laughed, saying, "Don't worry, gentiles can have some any time they wish." "What about Muslims?" I quipped. "Any time but Ramadan!"

On the way back to the house, 'D' was at first somber and quiet. Then, firmly, she commented, "It's a long reach for help." I wondered what she was thinking and asked. A moment later she responded, "Mossad has a couple of agents positioned to assist, except they are a long way from Long Beach! It will take some time to put things together!" She paused, then added, "My primary responsibility is for the children. But Mossad insists I serve their interests as well and the situation is evolving, rather rapidly, I'd say, to where I may need to be gone from time to time, lone wolf recon business, you understand!"

A moment later 'D' turned toward me cautioning that I should carry a weapon. And, if needed, to get a concealed weapon permit. I asked about her 9mm Beretta. Her response, saying it had a 17-round magazine, convinced me it would better suit my needs than the 12 gauge or 1911 .45 automatic with only five rounds. Elsje had a permit and carried it, especially in Jakarta. Her SIG Sauer P365 with 10 rounds with laser sighting for nighttime targeting was perfect. And, she is an expert marksman!

The night was twitchy. All past troubles, in Indonesia and here at home, were bent on parading through my inner vision, causing me to pace, stare out our bedroom French Doors, and watch, what could be seen in thin moonlight, scudding clouds displayed against a black sky, like ghosts ascending.

At about 3:00 am, while gazing at the yard below, Elsje whispered, "Grasshopper! If you don't get some sleep, you will be no good for yourself, or anyone else!" Without turning I muttered back, "You're right." I scanned the sky, then the yard, one more time, then crawled into bed, snuggled up to Elsie's back, and let faint fragrances of her hair shampoo carry me off to more pleasant scenes.

3

Hell Descending

With a barrage of activities, the week flashed by. First was a return to Disneyland. Terresa and Tommy insisted on seeing *Pirates of the Caribbean*, again! Rowland and Azra, along with 'D' did the honors, giving Elsje and me time to catch up with business matters, both here in Southern California, and Jakarta, and elsewhere where the Van Steenwijk Inter-Island Shipping Company had interests.

Elsje alerted the CEO and several vice presidents, ship captains, and operations chiefs in a conference call lasting over an hour. They energized an established security plan and notified local authorities who were charged with policing warehouses and waterfronts. I filed for a concealed carry permit and purchased a Beretta 9mm with four 15-round magazines. Sixty rounds should carry me through a firefight! On the other hand, praying I would not need to fire one shot!

The backyard was lovely. Our gardener, Roy Oshida, had made every planter, ornate pot, and shrubbery mass look perfect. The lawn was lush green. Afternoon winds were calmer than usual. Consuelo, assisted by Priscila, was busy preparing one of her favorite meals, tender lamb chops rolled tight and skewered, called a 'Saratoga', slow roasting in the barbeque. It was a fine meal. So pleased to see Rowland and

Azra and the kids, each healthy and happy. I just wish Sophia and Isabella could be with us. But it is their turn to complete university studies.

"Well, Rowland, if you feel like it, I would like to hear what happened down in Jakarta and Maputo." 'D' flatly said. Rowland sipped his lemonade, caught his breath, and then looked at Azra for confirmation. Azara nodded, saying, "We wanted the matter behind us and felt it best not to share when you came onboard 'D'. But, seeing how things are about, at least appear, to get bad again, it's best you know."

"I appreciate how sensitive this must be, for you both, but want you to realize, that in my capacity, it is much better to have as many facts as possible. For, I'm sorry to say, it would appear things may get rough!" 'D' politely responded.

Rowland took another sip, leaned forward, stared at the cedar decking for a few seconds, then said, "Mom mentioned what Dad related, taking of the ship Perseverance and all, so, I'll take it from there." Another sip of lemonade. Too fast I supposed for Rowland coughed a bit. But then continued, "After Azra and I were made aware, we talked over the situation in several calls back and forth, she at Oxford, and myself in Austin at the University of Texas. Also, we talked with Azra's folks, Eka and Adelia.

Rowland continued, saying, "We soon discovered we possessed assets, or had access to assets, Azra and I that is, that we could apply in helping. At least we thought it possible. Azra had access to diplomatic circles, some tight friends in high places, and sophisticated international research sources. I had access to computer technologies, plus, a few close friends. They are more than geeks, you understand; they are masters in computer sciences and programming. They had capacities our government, like CIA guys, wished they had. Anyway, we took about a month to sort things out, then, over a week, working long hours at my place in Austin, Texas, with loads of 3M sticky notes, pasted in my apartment, formed a plan!"

Rowland took another sip, then added, "Phase I was intelligence gathering! Phase II was remote intervention! Phase III was strategic actions. That last phase was the tough part for we would need to stay a step ahead of the bad guys while dealing with the diversities of reactions only discovered when and as they happened!"

"How many were you?" 'D' asked.

Azra responded, "The team included three girls; myself, and two friends, and Rowland enlisted three of his computer guys! Seven in all."

Rowland added, "We had code names. We never used our real names while communicating the whole time."

"You mind sharing your code names?" 'D' asked.

Rowland looked at Azra. She nodded consent. Then he responded, my guys were "PONG". "PAC MAN", and "ELITE"! Names of early computer games. "And yours?" 'D' inquired. Rowland grinned, saying, "KONG"! With a smile, Azra added, "Kong and Pong were our intrepid leaders!"

Azra then added, "Our code names were, "PANKHURST", FAUCETT, and, "WELLS", I am Wells. They are surnames of famous women leading the suffragettes in American politics during the late 1800s."

"So, did you have a name, or code for the team?" 'D' chuckled.

"We did!" Rowland responded. "Our team was called, "CONQUEST"!

'D', while shaking her head in amused amazement, asked Rowland to continue.

Rowland began again, saying, "Well, after forming the plan, Azra left for Maputo with her two friends. Pac-Man and Elite went to work hacking systems and tracking communication trails to discover, if possible, any pattern of conversations with keywords confirming our targeting the right guys. Pong and Kong (meaning myself) left for Jakarta to do some ground reconnaissance among some savory characters working the shipping docks. Our objective was to have all the basics we needed to establish phase one in a month's time."

Azra spoke, saying, "When we arrived at Maputo, my parents were dealing with some incidents of their own. Two vessels of our fishing fleet had been taken and the crews killed. All except three who were left for the sharks but survived and were able to describe the men and their vessel! They were certain it was Russians, their vessel, the 'Argo', was an attack vessel, the same as the Swedish Plejad Class with a 20mm cannon, machine guns, and torpedo launchers!"

Rowland picked it up, saying, "It was fast! We chased down the specifications and found it to be about 50' long and could do 37 knots top speed. The boat was listed as "stricken" in 1972 but the Russians got hold of it and did a complete refit." Then Azra said, "It was the best piece of intelligence that could have fallen into our laps!" Rowland quickly added, "Its electronics and communications systems gave us a digital signature we could surveil!" "And!" Azra added. "We were able, through my teammates, to identify ownership and operators of the vessel. It was owned by the Bratva mafia and operated by a skipper named Viktor Tolokonsky!"

Rowland took a long sip of his lemonade, then continued. "My guys in Austin went to work and soon we had names, locations, and dialogue trails needed, some cryptic, to be certain, but sufficient to begin putting pieces together. What we discovered was, just as Dad mentioned, we were dealing with Russian mafia working directly for the Russian government to establish a phony shipping system to transport arms and drugs, and insurgents, throughout Indonesia, southern India, and eastern Africa."

Azra then spoke, saying, "Pankhurst and Fawcett left for Ukraine with diplomatic credentials. Their objective was to identify key individuals and the organizational structure of the foul system the Russians were hoping to develop. They traveled to Belarus, Uzbeki, Georgian, Moldavia, and finally Turkman, and were able, after several close calls, and spending about twenty days in various meetings, gather and record other essential pieces of the puzzle."

"So, moving to phase two, I suppose, what happened?" 'D' asked. Then quickly added, "If I may, who was paying for all this activity?"

Rowland pointed at Elsje as Azara quietly said, "And my dad and mother."

Rowland continued, "We first began to hack Russian computers to disrupt and confuse them. It worked, to some extent. Then we began locating their thugs at various ports, the first being Port Moresby and the second at Jakarta and sent them confusing and contradictory digital encrypted orders using their passwords and codes. Local gang leaders were soon chasing their tails, going out to sea to nowhere and nothing, or various land locations that were empty shells or dead ends. This went on for another month and gave us a ton of information as to how they may respond and what assets they would use."

Azra spoke, saying, "It was not long after when hell began descending. They are smart, those Russians. They were able to reverse our computer attacks. We soon found ourselves on the receiving end of vicious Russian wolves, prowling our facilities in Jakarta, Durban, and Maputo. It was time to take action before they sent all their bloody soldiers into our homes and businesses. That's when Eka, my father, did something amazing.

"What did your father do?" 'D', nearly reverently, asked.

Azra nodded to Rowland who said, "It was not only amazing, but mysterious! Somehow, and we do not know for certain how, though we suspect it may have been through some Australians Eka met when Dad and the old German were sailing around the globe, secured two Ontos! And, a healthy load of high explosive, phosphorous, and armor-piercing shells, and training manuals by the United States Marines back in 1956.

"What in the world is an Ontos?" 'D' asked.

Azra answered flatly, "Tank killer!" 'D' jerked back in utter surprise.

Rowland continued, "It is technically listed as the M50 with six 106 mm recoilless rifles, that is to say, cannons, mounted on tracks and can do about 40 mph over rough terrain. But Eka didn't plan on using them on dirt, he mounted them on foredecks of two of his largest and fastest fishing vessels, disguised as storage boxes with tarps. He intended to take on the Russian fast attack boat, 'Argo' and blow it out of the water!"

"And?" 'D' excitedly inquired.

"Here is where things get messy!" Rowland commented. He looked at Azra who met his look with a wistful stare then nodded her head for Rowland to continue. Rowland looked at his mother who quietly said, "Perhaps there is a movie or two the children can watch. Then nodded for Priscilla to take Terresa and Tommy inside.

The kids were happy to do something more than listen to adults talk and bounded straightway for the house asking for Cinderella and Bambi movies. Consuelo refreshed the drinks and offered some light desserts on a large tray. The evening sky was clear and air balmy. And no mosquitos were around to pester.

After enjoying a few morsels of fresh Lemon Polentas, the story continued. Rowland, at first speaking with his mouth half full of desert, which brought a clearing of throat caution from Elsje, began by saying, "As Azra said, it was hell descending. We were openly attacked. First at Maputo, then our docks at Colombo, Sira Lanka, then at Jakarta, and even at the main warehouse where the corporate offices are located."

"Dutch Services joined local police at Jakarta and Sira Lanka. We repelled the Russians but cost the lives of at least three in Sira Lanka and another four in Jakarta. Among Russian henchmen, five died and six were wounded and arrested. In Maputo, Eka and his men were able to defend against a dozen mafia but lost two of their own."

Azra commented, "My dear friends, Pankhurst and Fawcett, were able to glean information from contacts in Belarus that Ivankov was aboard the Argo with a gang of thugs headed for Maputo. They were set on attacking my father's fishing fleet and taking over the business. Mozambique was still in a rage of civil war and we supposed they saw an opportunity to use the civil fighting as cover to get away with the takeover."

"That's when Interpol provided some assistance and was able to locate their fast attack ship. It was near Durban, South Africa, and headed for Maputo!" Azra continued.

"So, they were able to track the Argo by satellite?" 'D' asked.

"That's right!" Rowland responded. Adding, "It was through Interpol that Eka was able to do what he did with the two Ontos mounted on the foredecks of his boats!"

"How did that play out?" 'D' inquired.

"Well, while Pac-Man and Elite were doing their hacking thing in Austin, Pong and I flew to Maputo to help Eka. Each boat had a crew of ten men with automatic weapons, mostly AKs, and two Interpol agents with Canadian assault rifles and

HK 417 Sniper rifles. Teams of five men each were trained to operate the Ontos. Eka and I trained as well. It only required three men to manage the thing but we needed backup!"

"We set out early in the morning, knowing the Russians were off the coast about 23 miles. So we went as far as fifteen miles and set our fishing outriggers and gear. We knew they had radar so had us spotted. We knew also, from our radar, exactly where they were. It was a waiting game. And before long, they came. Not fast, but, well, almost like a tiger sneaking up on its victim."

"Eka ordered our vessels to position about half a mile apart and a few of the crew to go about normal fishing tasks. The Ontos crews were to be under the tarps covering the Ontos and be loaded, all 12 cannons, and ready to fire on the Argo when the command was given."

"I'm curious, what was the command?" 'D' asked.

Rowland looked at me, then his mom, and smiled, saying, "Well, it was borrowed from a command the old German used when dad, Eka and he sailed the South Pacific and fended off pirates. The command was "Hallelujah!"

Elsje and I laughed. 'D' smiled and shook her head. Then asked, "How did the Russians approach?"

"Interesting question, they came straight at us. They must have felt they were in complete control with the firepower they had and torpedoes they could easily launch." Rowland responded. Then added, "Our two fishing vessels certainly looked like sitting ducks, going about the work of fishing on the open sea. Sort of like old-time Caribbean pirates would say on a slow day, 'Let's go get a fat Dutchman!'" Rowland glanced at Elsje saying, "Sorry Mom!" He then continued.

"As they came, Eka slowly turned his boat, showing his port side to the Argo. Eka radioed me to do the same. I slowly placed my starboard side toward the Argo which was about three-quarters of a mile distant. You see, we had placed the Ontos to fire from our sides, not directly forward. Well, they kept coming at a modest speed and then used their megaphone and ordered us to prepare to be boarded. Saying, in rough English, "You have three minutes to get all crew on your foredeck and stop any movement! If you do not, we will destroy you!"

Azra spoke, saying, "My dad was an expert helmsman and could calculate time, distance, and angle with the accuracy of a Harvard math professor who knew the science of descriptive geometry."

"Absolutely!" Rowland added. Then said, "Half our crews were lying flat with their weapons on the deck. They were behind the gunnels so could not be seen. As I mentioned, the Ontos crews were already inside the tarps and ready to pull cords rigged to release the camouflaged Tank Killers in a flash. Then Eka used his megaphone and shouted, "What do you want with our poor fishing vessels?"

Rowland took a sip of lemonade and then continued. "I knew we had come to a critical alignment to fire on the Argo. I readily admit I was scared as hell as the Russians shouted back, "Do as I say or you die!" That's when Eka shouted, "Well, Hallelujah!"

"The tarps flew off and no more than two seconds passed when, 12 106mm cannons fired a volley of phosphorous, high explosive, and armor-piercing rounds on Argo. The explosions could be heard all the way back to Maputo. When the smoke cleared, we saw Argo's top side obliterated and in flames, and gaping holes in her side. There was a brief firefight but the Interpol snipers quickly dispatched their machinegun shooters as our crews unloaded, raking Russians with their weapons! Several leaped overboard in flames or to escape the flames. A few minutes later there were secondary explosions deep within their ship!"

"But the task was not complete." Azra quietly said.

"How so?" 'D' asked.

"They launched a speedboat off their stern and used the burning, sinking Argo as cover to get away! In no time they were out of range. But my father, with binoculars, had time to get a good look at the five or six men that boarded the craft." Azra added.

Shaking her head, 'D' spoke, saying, "No going down with the ship for those creeps!" Then asked, "So what about Eka, his death, and Ivankov?"

Rowland looked at Azara a moment, then cleared his throat, and said, "It was about ten days later. Eka was driving home from the Maputo office when he was abducted. They caught him in a tight street with no way to escape and burned his car. Then took him to an abandoned meat packing plant on the south edge of town near the waterfront. That is where we found him and the Russians, for some friends had seen the abduction, and two boys, on bicycles, followed the van carrying Eka to the place, and let us know.

'D' asked. "Was he alive when you got to him?"

"Barely!" Azra responded.

Rowland continued, "We called some of our people who rushed to the place. All ten or twelve of us arrived at about the same time. As soon as most of us entered the north doors, we heard screaming. It was Eka. They had him at the south end where they had hung beef slabs on hooks and rollers. Two of our people burst through the south door and were killed after they shot one of the Russians and wounded another. Then, just as we entered from the north side, the Russians ran and escaped in the van."

Azra was weeping and Rowland hesitated to continue. But Azra brushed tears aside, set her jaw square, and motioned for him to go on.

"The place was fairly dark and we, at first, could not see Eka. Then, just as our eyes adjusted, we heard a moan. Against the far wall, we spotted him. He was naked and had been lifted up with meat hooks in his chest. His body was sliced with a machete we found on the floor near a dead Russian. The Russian barbarians had sliced his body, on all sides, shoulders to his knees."

Rowland choked up and was unable to say more. Azra wrapped an arm across Rowland's shoulders and quietly said, "We got him down and just before taking his last breath, he whispered, "Ivankov, Dima, Alexi!" Then said, "Precious Adelia, my Adelia my Adel…" Then father died in my arms."

'D' stared at the deck, shook her head back and forth, and said nothing. Elsje wept as did I. For the loss of such a dear friend, such a sweet man, such an honorable and faithful man, was a terrible thing to bear.

Azra, speaking in words sounding like the growl of a lioness, said, "The day will come when Ivankov will be devoured!"

'D' looked up at Azara, and said, "By the God of Abraham, I will help you!"

A moist marine layer had suddenly made being out of doors less than pleasant. That, and sorrow of the account caused us to leave the deck and make our way inside, each carrying a load of dishes. Consuelo insisted she would do the work. We insisted otherwise. She smiled and muttered a happy Mexican salutation of appreciation.

The kids were slumped in chairs. Both nearly asleep. Priscilla was pleased to have watched Bambi and talked of *Flower* the skunk as being her favorite character. I scooped up Tommy and Terresa took her mother's hand as we climbed the stairs to their bedrooms. After seeing them to bed, 'D' paused in the hallway and whispered, "You have a wonderful family!" I smiled and whispered back, "I know." Then she said, "Pleasant dreams."

On the way to our bedroom, I pondered the fact. *How fortunate we are to have such a loving and close family.* Then, suddenly, as if a premonition had occurred, chills went down my spine as thoughts of evil people coming to harm my family caused my breath to catch.

In our bathroom, Elsje and I tried the typical talking while brushing our teeth, at best, a desperate experiment in garbled communication. With my final "What was that?" Elsje said, "Later, grasshopper!" and went to bed. I soon followed, slid in next to her, and asked, "Do you love me?" As did Tevye in *Fiddler on the Roof.* She turned to me, gave me a sweet kiss, and said, "Sharing a teeth-brushing session with you, dearest, is pure love!" I intentionally didn't say a thing for a moment. Then casually said, "Just wondered!" Then kissed her neck and snuggled close! For an hour or so, sleep was a restless reach. But, finally, scenes of the old German, Eka, and I, sailing Typee among incredible islands, held me in solitude with fresh silky sheets. That odd saying, *'Bed, the final frontier!'* was my last thought for a vexing evening.

4

Bag Lady

Work and play mixed nicely over the next few days. Terresa and Tommy wanted to go to the beach and build sandcastles as they had seen others doing. Their passive moments were spent scanning with binoculars from the day room with huge bay windows and skylights, fronting a portion of the house.

The kids had taken a fondness for Priscilla. She, being black, was thought of in warm terms of her ethnic kinship. In response, Priscilla was most intrigued about Mozambique which Terresa was anxious to tell, all she could, and more. Who knew, perhaps that's where Priscilla's ancestry came from? But as with most black people's ancestry in America, more than a few stone walls are all that is left.

"Oh my, look at that poor woman!" Terresa said to Priscilla. Priscilla got up from the floor where she had been playing Legos with Tommy and looked. "What woman?" Priscilla asked.

"There, sitting on that bench next to the stairs going down to the beach," Terresa responded.

"Oh, yes! Well, that woman is what some call a bag lady. There are many of them around, very poor and homeless. But usually, they ride transit buses to stay safe and out of the cold in winter. Don't often see them sitting on a street bench." Priscilla commented.

Around 6:00 that evening two men came to the front door. Priscilla answered. They asked for 'D', saying they were associates. Priscilla did not let the men inside, rather, she asked them to wait on the front porch, inviting them to sit on one of the lounge chairs. They politely nodded acceptance of the invitation.

"Did they mention names or show you identification?" 'D' asked Priscilla. "No mam, they just said you are an associate and asked for you," Priscilla responded.

"You did well by not letting them in." 'D' muttered as she walked toward the entry doors. When there, 'D' reached under her tunic and pulled out her Berretta. Then, cautiously, opened the door.

The two men stood, faced 'D' and bowed slightly, saying, with identification folders presented by each of them, "Agent 'D', I'm Cobi and this is Elam. We are here…"

"I know who you are and why you are here!" 'D' curtly said. "Please come inside, and, wipe your feet!"

The two men came into the foyer, gazed about, then slowly whistled their amazement at the wood parquet floor, Persian carpets, artworks, large oriental vases, tropical plants, and Asian teak furnishings. "Follow me!" 'D' said, motioning them as she walked toward the library. The library is a rather small yet beautifully appointed room with a Persian rug and leather chairs facing a partially stained-glass window looking over a small enclosed oriental garden. Hundreds of rare and famous books were neatly arranged with artifacts positioned here and there in counter-to-ceiling polished mahogany bookcases.

One dominant Rembrandt painting, a reproduction of Manasseh Ben Israel, a Dutch scholar and owner of a printing press, adorned the wall. He had printed the diaries of Christopher Columbus and other famous explorers. Intrigued by what he read in those accounts, Manasseh traveled to the Americas and returned to write, *The Hope of Israel*, a famous account of American native peoples, some of whom, he believed, were of Hebrew descent.

As they were staring, Elsje, followed by Azra, entered the room with Elsje saying, "The books, at least most of them, come from Acres of Books downtown. Hello gentlemen, I'm Elsje Schaffer and this is my daughter-in-law, Azra." Azra extended her hand with greetings mutually accepted all around.

Elsje then asked, "Would you care for some refreshments?"

"A cup of coffee would be nice," Cobi responded. Then he asked, "Is Rowland Schaffer about?"

"My husband is out back in the garage and storage room with the children," Azra responded.

"Would it be possible to talk with him a moment or two?" Cobi asked.

Azra looked at 'D' who nodded it would be okay. She left to get him. As she was leaving the room, Elsje said, "Have a seat. I'll get some coffee and, if you wish, some fresh banana nut bread." Elam, who appeared much younger than Cobi, instantly perked up, gave a bright smile, and said, "That would be great!" Cobi first frowned, then smiled, joining Elam in his enthusiasm.

Soon, Consuelo brought a tray and set it on a small table near where the men sat. Then Rowland, Tommy, and Terresa arrived, followed by Azra and Elsje with Tracey in tow. After introductions, Tracey suggested the living room would be a more suitable space for the conversation.

After settling in the living room, 'D' opened with, "These men, agents Cobi and Elam, are with Mossad and presently assigned to the Phoenix unit. They will be working with us to assist in dealing with the Russians as they begin making moves on your businesses and families."

Azra asked, "Mossad, Tele Aviv, Israel, they are supporting this endeavor?"

"Our assets are limited but, yes, headquarters is in support. And I will share with you, that this present danger you face is aligned with Israel's long-standing objective to bring down Bratva, and particularly Ivankov and his associates." Cobi responded.

"How do you think they will approach us?" Elsje asked.

"We may assume just as before. Likely the same as Rowland and Azra described the other night." 'D' offered.

"But there is new intelligence suggesting something more is working. Something we cannot quite figure out, as yet, but we're working on it!" Elam added. Cobi instantly gave Elam a stern look.

Tracey and Rowland caught the exchange and, almost in unison asked, "What more?"

Cobi looked at Tracey, then Elsje, and said, there are things we should talk about without children present. Teressa immediately stood up and complained, stating, "I'm not a child!" Not to be left out, Tommy stood and shouted, "I'm not either!" adding, "I'm a boy!" Then sat down. Azra gently ushered her children out of the room. As she did so, she whispered to Rowland, "Listen carefully!"

Cobi turned to Elam saying, "Go ahead, explain."

Elam took out a small notebook, glanced at it, and then tucked it away in his leather jacket. Clearing his throat, after having just swallowed a hefty chunk of banana bread, said, "As you know, Rowland, there is a woman who goes by many names, but to us is identified as Alina Volkov. She, as near as we can tell, and yet to be confirmed, is now in the Los Angeles area."

"The same as we saw in Dallas at the hotel?" Rowland asked.

"Yes. We believe the same!" Elam responded. Then added, "But there are two additional women, Russian assets, who entered the United States about ten days ago. One is Mila Galkin. The other, Galina Agapov. Galina is a specialist in kidnapping. Mila is skilled in drugging people and is a known assassin."

"Are you implying the Russians are after the kids? Tracey asked.

"Not necessarily, Mr. Schaffer. Actually, each of you is a prospect for kidnapping. You, your wife, Rowland, Azra, and the kids. We have no idea as to who. But, we sense, by all we can, at the moment assess, that the Russians have changed tactics and are going for ransom." Codi responded.

Looking directly at Elsje, 'D' added, "The ransom they may demand is your shipping company. Oh, they'll want money, alright. Lots of money. But, all things considered, they have not given up on a takeover of shipping in Indonesia and East Africa. They have too much invested." Cobi added, "Our European unit has confirmed this to be so!"

Elsje paled at the prospect. Taking a business is one thing. Taking family, especially children, is quite another. In a dark, pleading pulse of expression, Elsje muttered, "God in Heaven!" Then sorrowfully shook her head.

"Is there a plan?" Tracey asked.

"Not a complete plan as yet, sir, but we are close. That is one reason we came here today. We wanted to brief you and spend time with agent 'D' to work out details."

"Use my study!" Tracey flatly stated. Then added, "Take all the time you need and whatever, and I mean whatever you need, it will be provided!"

"Thank you, sir!" Cobi responded. Then he stood and quietly asked, "Would you and Mrs. Schaffer consent to fitting you, and your children, with transponders so that we may track your movements and be able to know where you are in the event…well, the event you are taken?"

Tracey looked at Elsje. She gave a slow nod back, her eyes welling with tears. 'D' moved close to Elsje, placed an arm around her, and whispered, "I can assure you we will do our very best to prevent it from ever happening." Elsje shifted her stance, looked at 'D', and said, "Most assuredly, if there be any assurance, protect my children!"

'D' invited Rowland to join them. With Cobi and Elam following, they moved to Tracey's study where communication resources, including the satellite phone, computers, and other business equipment could readily, with clever manipulation, be applied to the cause at hand. Rowland was ideally suited for the job.

In a matter of moments, Kong was in touch with Pong. Pong contacted Pac-Man and Elite. The team, *CONQUEST*, was reorganizing. Activated with the code word for urgent being "Hallelujah!" Then Rowland sent a message for Azra to join them. In moments she gathered her two assets together by satellite phone and now, Wells, Pankhurst, and Fawcett were activated. Azra turned to 'D' asking, "Now, agent 'D', what is it you want done? Adding, we are ready!"

Elam, with wide eyes, gasped, saying, "Holy Toledo!

Cobi quietly muttered, "If you two ever want to join Mossad, just call us."

They went to work. Hours passed and more coffee was brought to the study, along with slices of banana bread. Elam was pleased. The kids came by to kiss their parents goodnight. Then were taken to bed by Elsje.

It was not 3M sticky notes to help track and stage the plan, but a ream of printing paper coming off computers which finally, at about 2:30 am, revealed all the needed facts. The plan was formed by 4:00 am. All that was needed was for Tracey and Elsje to review and approve it. But that would wait until morning.

Priscilla had made separate bedding arrangements for the two agents in a spare guestroom with their own bathroom. There were four bathrooms, plus a powder room, in the house. Before the rise of morning street noises could disturb weary people, they quietly rested in the magnificent Schaffer abode on Ocean Boulevard. A home overlooking the Pacific Ocean and roughly 26 nautical miles away, Catalina Island.

"We have been there and done that!" Tracey growled as he handed the sketched-out plan to Elsje.

Elsje looked at the plan, looked it over briefly, and then said, "What my husband is saying is true. I was the bait. It was a dangerous procedure and I nearly lost my life in Sira Lanka." Then looking at Tracey, she added, "But is there any other way?"

Tracey looked at Elsje and said nothing. Then looked at 'D' and asked, "How confident are you that this will work?"

'D' flatly said, "In this rotten business, forced upon us by Bratva and the Russian government, there are no absolutes, no guarantees. But we have sufficient intelligence and capacity, with Mossad and your incredible kids, and others, to at least be assured, that an adequate defense will be in play!"

Tracey responded, "Sounds a little bureaucratic, 'D'!" Then he looked at Elsje and then at Azra and Rowland. Then back at 'D' and asked, "You mentioned transponders. What's that all about?"

Cobi responded, "It is a tiny transponder chip that attaches to the back of an earlobe. It works like a chameleon, that is to say, the chip changes to the skin color of the person wearing it. It can only be removed with an ultra-sound procedure. And, Mossad and other Israeli intelligence and defense services are the only ones with this technology."

"So it's not inserted under the skin?" Rowland asked.

"No!" 'D' responded. "It attaches with a special adhesive. It is so tiny that anyone seeing it will think it is a small mole. The person wearing it does not even feel that they're wearing the thing. And, we can follow a person by satellite!"

"So, the main part of the plan is to have Rowland and Azra be the goats, staked out for Russian 'lions' to sniff out?" Tracey commented.

Cobi responded, "That is correct. However, under tightly controlled conditions with electronic surveillance in play continually, and additional support when they are needed. And, you have the advantage of Rowland and Azra's 'Conquest' Team!"

Tracey looked tense-uneasy. He glanced again at Elsje, then Rowland and Azra. Then lowered his head saying, "I suppose it's all we can do, and hope to do." Then looking directly at 'D' Tracey firmly said, "I want you to be in charge of this operation. We know you well and you know us, especially the kids. You lead this thing 'D'! Okay?

'D' didn't even glance at Cobi or Elam. Looking straight back at Tracey and then at Elsje, 'D' responded, "Absolutely!" Cobi and Elam nodded in agreement. Then Cobi added, "'D' is the best Mossad agent we ever had and we miss her!" 'D' looked sharply at Cobi saying, "Oh shut up!" Then smiled.

With an uneasy consent to the plan, they went to work on details. Photos of the bad guys, and girls, had to be memorized. Strategies for taking the Russians down had to be fine-tuned. Weapons and ammunition needed for the operation, including vans, cars, and motorcycles for transport and getting away, needed to be acquired and staged. And, there was the need to establish stake-out locations where it would be most probable for a successful encounter.

After several options were thoroughly examined, including Century City, Marina Del Rae, and Newport Beach, the choice agreed upon was Seal Beach — specifically, the Seal Beach Pier and beach area. There are only three ways out. Highway 1, (The Coast Highway), Seal Beach Boulevard, leading inland, or Pacific Ocean.

The "goats" would be staked at the sandy beach up-coast of the pier. Observation points were plentiful. The pier, nearby shops and restaurants, and the beach itself presented clear lines of vision. Also, the jurisdiction was Orange County which was better suited with federal special response teams stationed nearby and sheriffs swat units.

It would fall to Rowland and Azra to go to Seal Beach and spend time at the pier and on the beach. Having a getaway, as it were, from the kids. The kids would remain at home with Elsje and Tracey and, Elam as support, just in case there was an attack on the house. Tracey and Elsje would be able to handle themselves well with the firearms they had at their disposal. Interesting thing, Priscilla confessed her knowledge of handguns. She had received training years before when seeking ways to defend against her abusive husband. Consuelo confessed also, saying, "I cook! You do dirty work!" Then muttered something in Mexican speak.

So, the stage, as it were, was set. The Conquest team, as well as Mossad, were busy monitoring the Russians. The equipment, weapons, and materials needed were acquired and in place. Local law enforcement units were briefed. And Interpol was alerted. The FBI was not engaged at all. "They have a keen habit of mucking things or doodling with their pathetic, self-serving, agency politics!" 'D' commented.

Three days went by. The weather was outstanding for beach activities. Rowland and Azra were having their measured, be it cautious, fun on the sand. Wading or swimming, visiting shops, or enjoying delightful foods provided by vendors and restaurants. But, actually, to them, it was becoming a delightful bore.

Intelligence indicated two additional male Russian thugs had entered the area but uncertain, exactly where they were. Undaunted, and hopeful the thing would soon be over, Rowland and Azra, again, mounted a fine Kawasaki motorcycle and headed the short distance away for Seal Beach. There were four Mossad agents ready at various positions. Communications were clear. Satellite surveillance was in fine order, feeding imagery back to stationed technicians in Tele Aviv. The transponders attached to earlobes were sending their bright signals to Tele Aviv, tracking every move.

At the Schaffer home, Elsje was in the kitchen helping Consuelo with a late breakfast. Tracey had gone to his lawyer's office downtown to address some business matters. Elam was in the library scanning the Wall Street Journal. Priscilla was upstairs making beds, cleaning bathrooms, and vacuuming floors. Roy, the gardener, was in the back working his horticultural magic with the landscape. Teressa and Tommy were in the front dayroom playing and scheming about how to convince their parents to go to Disneyland again.

"Oh look, Tomas!" Terresa whispered to Tommy. "It's that bag lady again."

Tommy looked, then turned back to his game, saying, "So!"

"I bet she is hungry!" Terresa said quietly, still gazing at the woman sitting on the bench. Then added, "Let's give her some money so she can get some food!"

"You give her some. I'm busy!" Tommy responded.

"Oh come on, don't be such a brat!"

"How much money?" Tommy asked.

"Oh, five dollars should do," Terresa whispered as she grabbed Tommy by the arm. The two ran upstairs and while on their way Elsje called out, "Breakfast in ten minutes children!"

"Be right there granmama!" Terresa shouted down the staircase.

They pulled a five-dollar bill from a case their mother normally carried. Then sneaked down the stairs, past the library where Elam had the newspaper in front of his face, and quietly out the front doors, down the sidewalk, and across the busy boulevard using the pedestrian crossing signal-lite, activated by pushing a button. Terresa, shouting over traffic noise to Tommy, said, "Wish we had those in Maputo!" Tommy shrugged in agreement.

Terresa and Tommy walked the short distance to where the bag lady, who had her head down, sat. Standing squarely in front of her, Terresa said, "We're sorry you are a bag lady and know you must be hungry, so here is some money for you to get food!"

The woman looked up at the children and smiled. As she did, her fake teeth, which made her look gross, startled Terresa. The lady said something that Terresa could not hear because of a sudden rush of traffic noise. She stepped closer and as she did, noticed a tuft of blond hair protruding from the woman's dirty gray hair.

Suddenly, Terresa stepped back, turned to take Tommy's arm, and said, "You're no bag lady, you are..." Then screamed as she felt Tommy being jerked from her hold and a man, with a mask over his face, slapped duct tape over Tommy's mouth. In the next instant, Terresa felt someone grab her from behind. Duct tape was slapped across her mouth. Then the bag lady took Terresa by the arm and injected a needle. The street, the bench, the beach suddenly spun around and around, and then Terresa felt her head slam into something hard as she was thrown into a van. Everything went black!

Just before it happened, Priscilla was upstairs cleaning in a forward bedroom. She had pulled up plantation blinds to dust a sill when she saw the kids being grabbed. She screamed. "lord no, lord no, oh lord no, no, no, no!" and ran downstairs, falling just before she got to the main floor. Elam was up and ran to help Priscilla. But she held up her hand and yelled, "They got the kids!"

Elam shouted into his communication device but then realized it was off. Fastened to his hip, the switch had caught on a button when sitting in the leather chair. He had no clue he was offline. Elsje came running!

5

Dark Fury

Rowland and Azra broke every speed limit and ran every red light navigating the motorcycle back to the house. They literally became airborne when crossing the bridge between Naples Island and Belmont Shores. Four agents, including 'D,' were right behind. Mossad was communicating the location of Terresa and Tommy, as they had been when the kids first left the house to help a bag lady.

"We're tracking them north on Redondo Avenue! Appears they're headed for the 405 Freeway, or, for Long Beach Airport!" The voice from Tele Aviv said.

"How fast?" 'D' shouted into her microphone.

"Slightly above normal speed." The voice responded.

"Got it!" 'D' responded. She contacted Elam asking, "What can you tell me?"

"Priscilla says it was two men and a bag lady. They have a green van. That's all she saw; no license numbers." Elam responded. "What the hell happened to you, Agent Elam?" 'D' shouted.

"They slipped out on me. Did not see or hear them. And, my system was off. Did not realize it. I must have caught the switch when sitting in the library chair!" Elam added, "I'm sick about it 'D', sick!"

"Make certain the house is secure. There may be additional attacks. Be certain Elam! Understand? Be certain!" 'D' flatly said.

"Got it!" Elam responded.

Just then the voice from Tele Aviv said, "We lost them! The blips on the screen just went blank!"

"What!" 'D' shouted. "How could that happen?"

"They've gone underground or, or, they may have wrapped the kids in emergency blankets with foil linings which can dampen or interrupt signals."

'D' turned to the agent driving the van and flatly said, "Get to the airport! Fast!" Then muttered, "Damn, they're going to fly those kids out of the country."

The driver jammed the peddle. The black van lurched, passing on the left and then right at racetrack speeds. They made the Coast Highway using what little shoulder lane space, for emergency vehicles, was available, passing cars and trucks as if they were standing still. After the Coyote traffic circle, they hit Redondo and raced north.

Five minutes later the Tele Aviv voice came back. "Think we have them again! Faint and intermittent signal but the only thing we have."

"Where?" 'D' shouted!

"They just passed under the 405 freeway at the northern end of Redondo Avenue and have entered the Long Beach Airport at, hang on, the Gulfstream Aerospace Corporation facility. There are several private jets parked there. Looks like one is positioned for exiting the containment area for a runway."

'D' called Codi who was in a separate car saying, "Get hold of Long Beach air controllers. Tell them to hold any private aircraft movement. Tell them it's a matter of kidnapping American children by foreign agents."

"Got it!" Codi responded.

"We lost them again!" The Tele Aviv voice suddenly shouted. The previous calm and collected tone of his voice was gone.

"Where were they when you last had them?" "Just past the Gulfstream…" Wait, wait, there is a plane moving. Looks like a Lear or Gulfstream!"

"We're almost there!" 'D' shouted back. Then she called to Codi asking, "Tell me you got the planes stopped!" Codi responded, "The idiot at the tower claims he'll need to confer with his supervisor!"

"Well?" 'D' shouts.

"His supervisor is visiting the throne! Said he'll try and talk with him in the men's room! "What!", 'D' shouts back, then turns to the driver and says, in a most desperate tone, "Faster!"

Just as their van careened through the Gulfstream parking lot, bounced over a planter filled with shrubbery, and burst through a fence onto the tarmac, a Gulfstream jet, set for take-off, began its run on a short runway south of the main runways. In seconds the plane was in the air then, at low altitude, banked sharply to the left, and headed south.

Standing on the tarmac, 'D' watched the plane until it passed into low clouds of an advancing marine layer. In sorrowful frustration, she whispered, "We'll find you. We'll find you; I swear we will!" Then she turned to see a string of security and police vehicles, lights flashing and sirens blaring, racing toward the van. Moments later, upon command by officers, 'D', her driver, and another Mossad agent, were kneeling on black asphalt, their weapons laid before them, hands up.

After all the explanations and bureaucratic verifications, 'D' and her team were released. At normal speeds, they headed for the Schaffer home. While on the way, the Tele Aviv voice returned on their transmitter saying, "We keep picking up intermittent flashes of a transponder. Our people say it is highly likely the kids were wrapped, head to toe, in security, or perhaps emergency blankets, and at least one of them is pulling it off their head, occasionally exposing the transponder, sufficient to give a signal."

'D' responded, "Do you have a flight trajectory?"

"At the moment, plotting several paths, they appear to be crossing Mexican air space at a southeast angle, flying at 40,000 feet at about 700 miles an hour."

"Any hypothesis for a destination?" 'D' asked.

Another voice responded. "'D' this is Matthew, sorry about the way things are going. Considering the Russian geo-political system in that region, there are three plausible destinations. One is Cuba, the other Venezuela, and the other, well, the other is anywhere in the Caribbean where drug cartels have a stronghold. Russians love working with snakes!"

"Perhaps, if it is one of the children pulling the cover down, and I would believe that is Teressa, we can, hopefully, get a more certain view of their destination over the next couple of hours." 'D' Responded.

"Will let you know!" Matthew affirmed. Then added, "Watch your back!"

At the Schaffer home, Azra stood at one of the bay windows staring at the empty bench across the street. Priscilla was standing silently in tears next to her. Azra put her arm around Priscilla's shoulder and quietly said, "You could not have known." "Yes, but I should have!" Priscilla responded. "I should've said something and didn't!" Priscilla could remain no longer and left for the seclusion of an attic room, her private quarters.

Rowland joined Azra at the window, the satellite phone gripped tight in her hand. After dialing some numbers and providing protocols, she said, "Fawcett, Pankhurst, dear friends, they've taken my children! I need everything you can dig up on the following Russians, Alina Volkov, Mila Galkin, and Galina Agapov! Yes, everything! From birth to present! Their parents, siblings, friends, schools, where they worked, and who they worked for! And, if possible, where they bank and their credit card information. What? Yes. Pac-Man and Elite are working on this as well and please coordinate with them. I will be here in Long Beach for a while longer and will let you know when I return to Mozambique. Yes Fawcett, what was that? What PMC are you referring to? Yes. I know one of their soldiers. They are one of the best! Yes, I hear you! I'll talk it over with Kong! Thank you, dear friends. Be careful! Thank you!"

'D' came into the room just as Azra was concluding her conversation with Fawcett and Pankhurst, and asked, "What PMC?"

Azra turned to 'D', her eyes red with sorrow yet fierce as a mother lion who had children taken by hyaenas, and flatly said, "Dark Fury!"

'D' looked surprised saying; You mean *DUNKLE WUT* out of Munich?

"Yes!" Azra sharply responded. *"DUNKLE WUT!* They are among the very best private military companies in the world and it is quite apparent we will need an extraction team capable of getting my children safely home!" Azra turned and peered out the window, staring at the street bench. Her eyes glistened with tears yet to fall.

'D' gazed at Azra, then at Rowland. Quietly she said, "You're right. You will need the best if they go where we think they may be going this very minute."

Azra turned sharply, looked at 'D', and asked, "Where?"

"Tele Aviv says they are 80% certain the plane is headed for Venezuela. Caracas, they believe!" 'D' responded.

Rowland grabbed the satellite phone from Azra and walked into the library. After shutting the door, he made a call to Pongo. His only words were, "Caracas, Venezuela, focus on Caracas!" Then he went back to join the others. Cobi arrived and they went into the living room to council together. There was no blaming or contention. They remained a team realizing there are things that can be wild radicals when devising strategies or plans. And among those things, for certain, are KIDS!

"So, it would seem we agree there are three things to consider!" 'D' said, after more than two hours of discussion; times, a rather energized discussion. "First, buying time with delay tactics. Second, logistics for extraction of the children, wherever they are, and third, elimination of any threat of retaliation by the Russians!"

When about to jump into details 'D' had a beep and took an encrypted message. After translating, and reading the message, a slow smile spread on a strained face. Looking at Azra and Rowland, she said, "It's Caracas! Outside the city about eight miles. Tele Aviv says they have strong signals again and know precisely where the kids are!

Azra released an excited 'eek' and threw her arms around Rowland. Elsje and Tracey embraced. Priscilla, who had returned and was standing at the living room door, bowed her head and quietly whispered, "Thank you, Jesus!"

It was determined that Azra and 'D' would fly to Munich and engage DUNKLE WUT for the extraction. Tracey and Rowland, along with Cobi and Elam, would hunker down and deal with whatever demands the Russians may make. Elsje had many issues to address with the Van Steenwijk Interisland Shipping Company and needed to go to Jakarta.

"Are you ready for this?" Rowland asked Azra outside her boarding station at LAX. "Are you?" Azra responded. Her beautiful face was tight with emotion. Neither one said another word. They held each other…tightly held each other. Then Rowland whispered, "I love you!" Azra responded, "We will be together again…all of us." Then she, and 'D', who was standing nearby, boarded the Lufthansa redeye flight for Germany.

Two days later, Elsje and Tracey were saying their adieus near the same terminal but for Elsje it was KLM's 747 to Hong Kong, then on to Jakarta. "They are going to demand everything, you know that!" Elsje said.

Tracey thought a moment then responded, "They'll get nothing! Nothing that is but the rath of a lioness!"

"Few know her capabilities, her training and athletic skills, even deadly skills," Elsje said with a wry smile. Adding, "Her beauty and wit is like a sniper's camouflage."

"Soon, very soon, they will! God help those Russians when Azra attacks!" Tracey whispered.

Nearly unwelcome, the call to board came loudly. They embraced, kissed, and held each other's hands until space and access controls at the gate separated them. Elsje turned and lip-synced, "I love you!" then disappeared down the ramp.

On the way home to Long Beach, Tracey received a call from 'D'. She was with Azra in Munich and was about to meet with Dunkle Wut. Then she said, "Tele Aviv has isolated the location of Teressa and Tommy. They are in a mansion located near the town of Macuto, Vargas, on the coast. The villa is the headquarters of a drug cartel known as, Cartel de los Soles, or Cartel of the Suns! They are embedded with the Venezuelan military and totally ruthless!"

"So, what's the problem? Tracey responded.

"This operation is going to require more than an extraction team. We will need heavy coverage from your United States

Navy or Coast Guard to ensure recovery and escape from Macuto. Can you help arrange it?"

Tracey thought a moment. Then responded, "You can count on it 'D'! I have the contacts we need and will call in a marker!"

"Great!" 'D' responded. Then said, in a few moments I will send a link with satellite imaging of the Villa. Be back in touch after this meeting!"

When he arrived home Tracey went straight to his study where Codi, Elam, and Rowland were busy with three computers, digging out information. "They are at Macuto, Vargas, on the coast, outside Caracas!

"Right Dad!" We have it here on screen! Rowland said. "Have a look! It looks brutal!"

As they looked, Codi commented, "This Cartel is actually part of the Venezuelan military and has access to all assets their ruthless government holds!"

"What about this Dark Fury, can they do the job? Tracey asked Codi.

"They certainly have the best people and assets available," Codi responded.

"I asked, can they do the job?" Tracey growled. Then added, "Or do they need support?"

Codi looked at Tracey, then at Rowland, saying, "Best if they had support! But from whom?"

"That's all I need to know. I'll handle the 'who' part!" Tracey calmly said. Then took another look at the Villa image on the screen, grabbed the satellite phone, and went to the library, shutting the door behind him.

"Hello Elizabeth, this is Tracey, is there any chance I can speak with him for a few moments?" Tracey said on the phone.

"Well, I'll be! How are you? Where are you?" Elizabeth responded.

"At home in Long Beach. We have a major crisis and I need his help. I wouldn't even think of calling unless…"

"I know. I know, Tracey. You don't need to apologize. I will see if he can talk. He's somewhere over Ohio at the moment on 'One' but I'll let him know and get back to you."

"You don't know how much this means to Elsje and me! Thank you!"

"Don't worry. Please say hello to, Elsje and the kids!"

Tracey went back to the study and was going through the intelligence Pong, Pac-Man, and Elite had garnered and was talking with Codi and Elam about response strategies to ransom demands when the satellite phone chimed.

"Tracey Schaffer," Tracey answered.

"Well, how's that boy of yours doing after being put through the strainer at the University of Texas? I hear he is in, where, Mozambique, doing some fishing!"

"Good to hear your voice, Mr. President. Rowland is here with me and waves a greeting."

"Liz said you have a problem. How can I help?"

"The grandchildren, Terresa and Tommy, have been abducted by Bratva. Our businesses in Jakarta and Maputo, and here in Southern California are being attacked, and the Russian Mafia are having a field day!" Then Tracey added, "The kids are sequestered at Macuto, in a Cartel Villa near Caracas, Venezuela. Mossad is helping."

"Good lord Tracey! Had no idea. What do you need?"

"Azra is with a Mossad agent in Munich working on arrangements with Dunkle Wut for extraction. We know success will depend on escape, Frankly, G. W., we need the Marines!"

"Dunkle Wut teams are the best! Well, second to our Seals. I'll make a call and get you what you need! We'll help get your grandchildren safely home! Expect a call within the hour. And, my good friend, take care!"

Tracey clicked the receiver, terminating the call. Codi and Elam sat in oblivious wonder. They were hesitant to even ask. Noticing their stupor, with a wry smile, Tracey said, "Old friend! We made him president of The United States!"

The meeting with Dunkle Wut began. The president, his secretary and chief of operations, and two mission planners were there. Sitting there as well was one of Azra's friends who, also, was from Mozambique. She was an extraction team member and had been with Dark Fury for three years.

"We have your brief agent 'D' and have looked at options. Your latest intel presents an issue that has the potential of becoming a hurdle too high to jump!" The president of Dunkle Wut continued, saying, "What are your options?"

'D' flatly responded, "We are aware of that possibility and have requested support. If we are focused on the same matter, it is escape from the Cartel Villa and getting out of the country! Correct?"

The operations chief spoke, saying, "Yes, and that depends a great deal on the take-down of the Ivans, and Cartel thugs. It is a matter of how many are left standing." Then added, "However, if they are not able to call for support, we'll have the whole Venezuelan Army and Air Force to deal with, and that, ladies, presents a serious problem!"

Azra spoke, saying, "We are working to fill the gap and close that issue! Of that I am confident!" Her steeled clarity and voice tone grabbed the attention of all present.

After a brief silence, the president leaned back in his executive chair and asked, "Mind elaborating?"

At that very moment, 'D''s phone beeped. She apologized as she scanned the caller identification, then said, "Excuse me, gentlemen, I must take this."

"Yes, yes I understand. Really! Incredible! Thank you, sir!" Then 'D' placed her phone back in its case. She then turned to the president and said, "The Chief of Naval Operations for the United States has authorized, under direction by the President of the United States, to provide support!" Details will be conveyed in coordination with your operations chief!" Then she smiled a wry smile and added, "Does that help?"

They gawked at each other for a second or two. The president leaned forward, looked at his operations chief, and said, "Put it together!" He got up and was about to leave when Azra stood, looked at the man, and said, "There is one thing!"

The Dark Fury president stopped and looked at Azra. Then asked, "What is that?" Azra responded, "I'm on the team!"

"What! The operations chief shouted! No way!" Others sitting there, all that is except Azra's friend, began chuckling. One spouted off saying, "This ain't no rose garden party sister!" Another, somberly, said, "We'd be bringing you back in a body bag if there was anything left of that beautiful body (his eyes ogled up and down Azara), left to carry!"

'D' held her hand up stopping what was becoming an increasingly impolite protest. Having their attention, and after the president re-took his seat, 'D' said, "Gentlemen, allow me to define Azara. First, she is a descendant of The Lion of Gaza, King of all Eastern Africa, and has more education than any three of you put together. Second, she holds a 10th-degree Wushu and is a black belt in three other Korean and Chinese combat arts. Third, she is an expert with several firearms, including machine guns. Fourth, Azra holds several titles in fencing and was a member of the British Olympic Fencing Team. And, gentlemen, she has one other qualification none of you possess and never will!"

"Dare we ask!" The president quietly said. "Azra is a mother of two children, abducted by some of the most evil and despicable people on the planet. You would be fools to challenge her resolve!" 'D' leaned back in her chair, sat quietly, and soberly stared at the men. There was silence.

The president looked at his people, and they at him. Then he said, looking at Azra, "If your great grandfather was the Lion of Gaza, then you, lady, must be the Lioness! Welcome to Dark Fury!" Each of them shook her hand, even the operations chief who, leaning toward Azra whispered, If I may say so, madam, "You're the most beautiful lioness I've ever seen!"

6

Extraction

The contract was signed. All assurances were made. It was Team Seven, the best extraction team Dunkle Wut had. There were eight men and three women. One of the women was Azra, then 'D', the other, Sharmila, Azra's long-time friend, and herself a black woman. In her Mozambique tongue, the name means *protection*.

They had code names. It was letters and numbers, like A1, B2, C3, and so forth. Azra was given L3. Sharmila had G6, and 'D' was issued K2. Everyone was an expert in their daring and deadly vocation. Each was in top physical condition. Azra, however, knew what she needed to do, admitting to 'D', "I'm a bit behind but will catch up!" They had 15 days to plan and prepare.

In Jakarta, Elsje had the company in excellent operations throughout Indonesia. There were some minor incidents at Port Moresby and Sri Lanka, but they were dealt with quickly, dispatching two Russian mafia agents. "They attempted to sabotage one of the engines of the ship! And, were spying on our operations at the Sri Lanka port!" Elsje said to Tracey in one of several phone calls. During one such call, she repeated the question asked several times before, "Have they revealed their demands?"

Tracey responded, "Yes! Just an hour ago! They are demanding complete control of Van Steenwijk Inter-Island Shipping and two million US dollars in cash! One million for Terresa and another for Tommy!"

With an uncommon slur, Elsje coughed in anger, then said, "Tell them the transfer of ownership of the company will require a ton of red tape and adherence to international maritime registration and shipping laws! Tell them also, that our vendors and clients, from Australia to India are aware of their tactics and they will encounter shipping, docking, and loading issues that suffocate any operations they hope to attempt!" Elsje more calmly added. "Anything else?" I mean are there any delay tactics that will work on these clowns?" Tracey responded.

"Yes!" Elsje said, "Tell them Interpol, Dutch Security Services, and every law enforcement agency from Australia to East Africa are watching their moves! Problem is," she added, "Many of those same agencies are corrupted by the Russians." Then, in frustration, she said, "The whole world seems to be going down that path...corruption! Top to bottom!"

"Hang in there girl!" Tracey offered. "If there is a way, and I believe there is, we will make it through this. Besides," Tracey added, "The United States Navy and Marine Seals have joined the effort!"

"What!" Elsje shouted. How did that..., oh, you called him! You called, didn't you!"

Tracey was silent a moment, then said, "Yes, sweetheart, I had to. Saw no other way to make this thing work in

Venezuela. And, GW remembers well the help your dad and your family here in Long Beach provided during his service as a Senator, and long before he became VP and, President. He is a great and faithful man and did not hesitate to assist."

Elsje was silent a moment. Then said, "Navy and Marines, huh! Sure you didn't enlist in the Air Force as well?"

"Didn't need to. The Navy and Marines can handle it well, along with Dunkle Wut…and our secret weapon, CONQUEST!" Tracey shot back.

"When does it happen?" Elsje asked.

"Can't tell and would not tell sweetheart. You know the protocols. But when it does happen, and we are certain of their safety, then it will be one word!" Tracey was about to say the word but Elsje jumped in front of him and shouted, "Hallelujah!"

"That's right babe, hallelujah! God willing!" Tracey soberly said.

"Yes…God willing!" Elsje slowly responded.

"The mission is extraction! The packages are two children, Tressa and Tommy Schaffer. Teressa is 13 and Tommy is 10; study their images well. The target is a Villa in Macuto, Vargas, Venezuela. It is occupied by the Cartel de los Soles and is the residence of their leader, Ramos. Here are shots of him and his family. Note that among his children there are a boy and a girl about the same age as Teressa and Tommy. Study the compound, for it is a compound, even if it looks like a palace in a tropical garden. There will be every kind of defense and audio/video device available to detect and reject intruders. And we, gentlemen, and ladies, are the intruders."

The operations chief then asked if there were any comments or questions. None were offered. He then motioned to the team leader to continue the briefing.

"Listen up!", team leader, 'S1', shouted "Insertion will be by C-130 Hercules flying into the country from the southeast at low altitude, then over the mountains crossing their National Park, El Avila, then down the northern slope to the drop point. You will be jumping in black paraglider gear at a low altitude with night vision. Your drop zone is this small field with the two sheds shown here, just beyond the line of trees east of the Villa about 200 yards! The advance team will have planted a transponder in the field to guide us in. Please, boys and girls, try to miss the sheds!" Everyone chuckled.

Team Seven had been at it for days. They were at it again, going over every detail of the villa, positions of Cartel soldiers, and entry and exit points. The two red blips on a screen, transponders on Teressa and Tommy, kept in adjacent rooms, were still showing bright. But yet, another full rehearsal was held with the team leader, S1.

"The advanced team will be J5, M8, and Q10! They will insert as part of a tourist excursion two days in advance and provide real-time Intel. As you know, the main body of the team will insert by paragliding into the target area, landing at precisely 2:30 am on the 12th. Conquest tells us that the night before there is a large party to be held for military leaders with all the typical Latino libation and frolic! We can hope it is a lot of libation!

"Conquest also confirms they can electronically, and remotely, disrupt power at the Villa and shut down all internal communications for about one hour. They will also jam military radio frequencies and can assure us about 30 minutes, perhaps more, for a communications shutdown among Venezuela's finest.

"That means, folks, extraction must be complete in 30 minutes. At 3:00 am the packages must be secured and on their way to the exit point, which is right here at the Caraballeda Marina, about 1.7 miles from the Villa." The operations chief slapped a pointer on the large map showing nearly every detail of the Landing Zone, the Villa, the route to Caraballeda, and a small boat basin on the opposite side of the marina.

Azra stepped forward and took a long look. Then asked, "How certain are we that they are on the second level of the villa?"

"The advance team is charged with confirmation. However, we have established reasonable certainty they are on the second level in connected rooms but kept separate from each other." The operations chief responded.

Azra looked squarely at the operations chief and said, "Reasonable certainty?" Then turned away and stared at the screen where two red blips remained stationary.

Two days later a gathering of the team for a final briefing was held. "We will exit by the east end of the Villa compound at 3:00 am. That is where the advance team will have two vans waiting. The way to the exit point is marked on your GPS system. Another team of three will be waiting at the Caraballeda Marina with a high-speed vessel cloaked as a fishing boat. They will be positioned at Laguna Beach basin near the end of the boardwalk where all will board and exit to Tortuga Isle," the operations chief said. After slugging down some coffee he continued.

"The rumb line for Tortuga will take us to Punta Arenes at the west end of the island. It is 107 miles from Caraballeda to Tortuga. At about 30 knots boat speed we should make the crossing in 3.5 hours. Perhaps sooner. On station will be an American submarine. At this time of year, we should connect with the sub just before daybreak."

"Now, as for engagement: From all we know, Bratva soldiers are heavily armed and committed to barbarism, and, make no mistake, proficient at it! Likely the same for the Cartel junkies. No quarter is to be given. Take them down, get the packages, and get out! Understand! And, hope those Latinos have consumed all the liquor they desire!"

Then, with a stern look at each member of the team, he said, "Any questions?" At first, no one responded. Then 'D' raised her hand saying, "I have had a request from Mossad." "What request?" S1 asked. "Actually it is an order. I am to take any opportunity to terminate Ramos, the leader of Cartel de las Soles!"

S1 looked at 'D' for a second, smiled, and then said, "Seems you and I have the same instructions K2. Want to flip a coin for the privilege?"

"No way, S1, you Germans like using two-headed coins!" 'D' responded. Everyone chuckled.

S1 nodded, smiled, then looked squarely at Azra, smiled again, and said, "Let's bring those children home!" A robust cheer erupted, all the team looking at Azra. Azra, at first, sat still as stone, then nodded and quietly said, "Thank you." In her own way, she was extending an obvious and deep appreciation for the skills and dedication of Team Seven. All of them knew it.

The three women, L3, G6, and K2, departed for a private dinner together at one of Munich's finest restaurants, Le Stollberg. There were three days left before they left for South America where they would stage the extraction at a remote airport outside Guayana City, in Guayana. All things considered, even the weather, the extraction was on!

"Hello Kong! L3 misses you terribly!" Azra said, her ear tight to the phone.

"Kong is going crazy without you L3!" Rowland responded.

"The party is on. Cannot say exactly when, but soon, very soon!" Azra said.

"So wish I could be there!" Rowland responded.

"Are you set to party?" Azra asked. "Absolutely!" Rowland responded.

Then Rowland added, "No worries, Kong and Pong are ready for the games and Pac-Man and Elite are willing partners for the dance! All waiting for that magical word!"

"Perhaps you guys can tune in. Be sure the brightness knob is turned up on your screen!" Azra said with a slight chuckle. Then, for a moment, there was silence between the two. Finally, Rowland quietly said, "Love you L3!" "Love you Kong!" Azra responded. Then she slowly turned her phone off. They both knew it was blackout time. No more exchanges unless there is a crisis. No more talking until that magical word for success is heard.

"Two minutes!" The co-pilot announced to the team. They stood, clustered in two groups, they checked each other and began the walk to the ramp, slowly opening over the mountains of Venezuela. Ahead of the C-130 were the bright lights of Caracas. Behind the plane all was blackness. Mountain jungles descending northward toward the sea.

S1 turned and shouted, "Remember low altitude! It's a ten-count drop, then pop chutes! It's going to be a long glide! See you on the ground! A united, vigorous shout, "Hurrah!" echoed throughout the cavernous belly of the plane. Each member rehearsed in their mind the Intel reports that came while staging at Guayana the night before.

"J5 to S1! We have confirmed twenty-three soldiers on the grounds and verandas of the villa. By the imagery we are transmitting, you'll see three positioned at the service entry, and point of exit, on the east side. Twelve are at key points on the grounds, including the main gate, and eight are positioned at key locations on the villa. The wall is eight feet high with a high-voltage electric wire running along the top. And, we have spotted two guard dogs!"

"S1 to J5, how about the interior and the packages?" J5 responds, "Body heat imaging confirms ten soldiers in the interior. Eight are clustered in and around the main amusement hall. Two are positioned close and move with Ramos. There are about a dozen servants. Packages are on the second level, twenty feet from the west wall. They are in separate but adjoining rooms. We detected one person with each package and another coming and going. Not certain but best believe they are female."

"S1 to J5, is the locater set in the field?" J5 responds, "Set and operational!"

"S1 to J5, see you at the extraction point. Good work! S1 out!"

In silence, the team descended. The transponder in the field left no doubt as to the exact landing zone. But it was a long way and every skill in navigating their paragliders safely to the ground was required. As seconds flew by, it was looking slim to be able to make the LZ. S1 radioed the team, saying, "If we're short, make your way as quick as possible to the transponder. We'll gather there! Good luck!"

Azra whispered to herself, "We're going to be way short!" She glanced at 'D' who was gliding to her right, then Sharmila, who was about fifty feet to the left. In silence, they each shook their heads, recognizing there may be a serious problem. Perhaps a half-mile short problem.

Not more than ten seconds later, an updraft, a light and steady puff of wind rushed from the sea up the mountain slopes. The relieved paragliders soared and adjusted. In an instant, nature, or providence, perhaps both, salvaged the mission from becoming very complicated, if not a total failure.

Three minutes more and eight sets of Dark Fury boots were on the ground. No one collided with the two shacks. No injuries! S1 and the rest of the team checked the time. It was 2:23 am. They had seven minutes to breach the service gate and begin to execute the extraction. Each one knew their part in the play. Azra and 'D' were behind S1, B3, and G9, who took point. G9 was the smallest yet most agile of the team. He had all the skills of a Ninja and more! In absolute silence, he dispatched two of the guards with knives thrown from about thirty feet.

B3 swooped inside the gate, past G9, and dispatched another guard who was tilted back in a wicker chair outside the guard station. In a single movement with a lariat around the guard's throat, the guard was done. The only sound was like a slight cough as the guard slumped to the ground. Then B3 ripped out communications and alarm wires, gathered walkie-talkies, and tossed them outside the wall.

At that same moment, as Conquest promised, lights went out all over the grounds and in the villa. In seconds the entire team was inside the villa compound. About fifty feet in, behind palm clusters and shrub masses, the team knelt and scanned the area with night vision headgear, selecting targets. There were five in fairly close range. On a down-count of three, each assigned team member, their weapons fitted with silencers, took down a target. Eight of the soldiers, be they Russian or Cartel boys, didn't matter which, were instantly dispatched.

Like an energized lizard, G9 climbed a pillar to the second level of the villa. He anchored and tossed down a rope and was about to signal K2 and L3, 'D' and Azra, to climb up. Suddenly he held his hand to signal caution, turned, and fired on a very surprised guard who had walked around the corner holding a flashlight. With a groan, the guard dropped to his knees, then flopped forward, stone dead! G9 then motioned L3 and K2 to climb.

At the second level, L3 and K2 entered through French doors and made their way to a long hallway leading to the west end of the villa. There was snoring, liquor-soaked snoring, bodies everywhere. Tiptoeing through them was fairly easy with night vision. However, several were obviously in light slumber and could be easily disturbed. One, half sat up, looked right at L3 and K2, mumbled something in Spanish, then laid back down.

Once in the wide hallway, they were nearly trotting to the west end but suddenly stopped when two young women left a room gripping the rail leading them downstairs. They were hot-to-trot in visiting a couple of guards anxious to see them. The stairs were open and wide with a curve leading to a huge foyer. As L3 and K2 were slowly inching across the opening, a distance of twenty feet or more, one of the guards flashed his flashlight up nearly blinding them. In a flash, with their night goggles tilted back, 'D' and Azra dropped the guards and the two girls. Then ran for the rooms where Teressa and Tommy were. Just as they got to the rooms, loud dogs barking and men yelling, with rapid bursts of automatic gunfire erupted outside.

A door, just behind where L3 and K2 thought the kids were kept, burst open. There, standing in a nightshirt, was Mila. She had a flashlight trained on Azra and raising a pistol was about to fire, when two quick thuds were heard. Mila fell. Standing behind her was G6, Azra's friend. Together, the three women advanced to the bedrooms where Teressa and Tommy were kept. L3 opened the first door. On the bed sitting straight up, was Teressa. Overcome with emotion,

Azra lunged for Teressa. Just as she got to her, Terresa screamed! She pointed off to the opposite side of the room, then screamed again.

Out of the dark, Galina pounced on Azra with a knife. Before Azra could respond, Galina wielded a stroke across Azra's face. Azra jerked back but the tip of the knife caught Azra at her left eyebrow, nicking her upper cheek but missing her eye. With blood dripping down her face, Azra grabbed Galina by her arm, wrenching the knife from her hand, then flipped her so hard Galina crashed through a window, landing on the veranda. Tearing a strip of material off a pillowcase and holding it to her eyebrow to stop the bleeding, Azra scooped up Teressa saying, "Let's go sweetheart!"

There was more and more gunfire outside. Several rounds crashed through what was left of the window. K2 had Tommy who had been in the room Mila emerged from and was under the bed when 'D' finally found him. "Get to the exit!" L3 shouted. Tommy, casually said, "Hi Mom!"

K2 shouted to G6, "Take Tommy! I've got a task to complete! Azra shouted, "Let it go!" But 'D' was down the stairs, headed for Ramos. Azra and G6 ran down the hall and were about to the place where they could exit the east end and get to the exit point when Alina burst out of a room in front of them. Teressa screamed, "Bag lady!"

Alina had an automatic rifle, an AK 47, and was about to fire when a drunken Venezuelan soldier fell out of the same room, blabbering in Spanish, "What in hell's going on?" He collided with Alina, knocking her against the wall. Losing grip on her weapon, it slid along the polished tile floor to where Azra and Teressa stood. Teressa instantly picked it up.

Alina stood, frozen. Her mouth gaping open. Teressa slowly raised the weapon and flatly said, "You're disgusting!" Then fired nearly ten rounds. Alina's body was blown backward, sliding nearly to the end of the hall. Azra looked at G6. At first in amazement. Then, looking at Teressa, she smiled, saying, "Let's Went!"

They made the veranda. Then down to the ground, courtesy of S1, C8, and D7 who held a tarp like a fireman's catch. Just after they jumped, Galina, bloodied from head to toe, from crashing through the window, shouted a curse in Russian. She was leaning over the rail with a weapon in hand. She straightened stiffly and was about to shoot when B3 fired a burst from behind. Her body flipped over the rail and crashed to the ground, at the feet of Azra and her children. Terresa, and Tommy, in unison, spit on her near lifeless body. She muttered another foul curse, then gasped and died.

The automatic weapons fire had stopped. S1 asked, "Where is K2?" "Taking care of business!" L3 responded. S1 smiled. Then said, "Get to the vans, I'm going to get her.

S1 ran around to the front doors of the villa. Several bodies were strewn along the way, including the attack dogs. The team was exiting fast. Two rushed past S1 shouting "All down and clear!" S1 ran into the foyer just as K2 was coming out of a hallway on the main floor carrying two large satchels. "You good?" S1 asked.

"Fine, just fine!" K2 responded, tossing one of the satchels to S1.

"Well let's get the hell out of here!" S1 quietly said.

As they ran for the east gate S1 asked, "Did you get Ramos?"

"Oh yes!" 'D' responded with a wry grin.

Just as they got to the van, S1 asked, "What's in the satchels?"

"I'm guessing about two million in $100s and $500s, US!" K2 flatly responded.

"Holy sauerkraut!" she shouted as 'D' threw the satchel and herself into the van. S1 quickly followed and yelled, "Go, go, go!" It was 3:01 am. They were on their way to the marina at Caraballeda.

At the Laguna Beach boat basin, the camouflaged vessel was waiting. Two of Dark Fury's warriors, specialists in handling watercraft, were near the dock doing something on the bank. The team piled out of the vans and ran for the boat. S1 hollered, "What's happening!" "Two cops became suspicious and we had to take them out!" One shouted back. The other added, "One may have got a message off on his radio!" S1 shouted. "Leave it be and let's get out of here!"

The team quickly stripped off the painted canvas camouflage revealing a high-speed craft of the type drug transporters use in the Florida Keys and Caribbean to try and outrun the US Coast Guard.

"Take your kids below, L3! Safer there!" S1 shouted as the boats' engines roared to life. Soon they were gaining speed, maneuvering past other vessels as they raced out to sea. Another team member had binoculars, watching the Caraballeda marina and shoreline. Not a minute went by before he shouted, "We have company!" S1 raised his binoculars and confirmed the situation, saying, "Looks like one of their more modern chasers. They have machine guns mounted on those puppies!" Then, after a longer look, said, "Hunker down folks, they're not giving up!"

Suddenly, flashes from the chase boat could be seen. Tracer bullets were flying everywhere around them. A few hit the boat but were not damaging. Two team members fired back. Then ducked as a volley of fire came from the two deck-mounted machine guns. The driver of the Dark Fury boat was turning back and forth, evading as best as possible. In frustrated anger, Azra started up the ladder to join the firefight. Sharmila stepped in front of Azra saying, "No, sister, we've got this. You belong with your children." In that same instance, just as Sharmila was about to say more, two sickening thuds were heard. Sharmila got a surprised look on her face. Then she groaned and slumped to the deck.

Azra grabbed Sharmila, and pulled Sharmila's head up to her chest pleading, "No! No! No!" But she was dead. Suddenly, Azra jumped up, brushed by 'D', and stood on the deck near the stern, screaming at the chase boat. Then she turned and shouted at their driver, "Slow down a little!" Looking about, she pointed saying, "Give me that stovepipe!" A team member threw off a tarp covering an M9 Bazooka. Azra looked at it a second, then Shouted to the team member, "Load it!" Then said, "Now get out of my way!" Everyone ducked for cover.

Hoisting it to her shoulder, she sighted the Bazooka, whispering, "Closer you scumbags…closer, closer!" A few seconds passed as she leveled the M9, took a breath, then fired. A trail of solid rocket propulsion lit up the night sky. But not as much as when it struck the Venezuelan chase boat. The explosion was horrific. A huge fireball filled the humid air. Setting the bazooka down, Azra looked at the team member who had given her the Bazooka and said, "Thank you!"

The team let a hardy cheer, shaking fists at a demolished pursuer. Then all attention turned to Sharmila who had been carried below and was being carefully wrapped in a canvas tarp by 'D', with Terresa helping. Azra sat next to where Sharmila lay and spoke softly in her native Mozambique. Covering her face, as she sobbed.

Teressa and Tommy placed their arms around their mom's shoulders and together sat in somber silence: silence over the reality, and miracle, of being together, and the loss of a dear friend. The only Team Seven member lost on the mission.

While a medic was treating the Azra's cut, S1 and K2 were talking. "So, how did it go down?" S1 asked 'D'. "Well, it was strange. Ramos stumbled out of his bedroom in skivvies, each hand holding a polished silver pistol, and shouted, 'What the hell's happening?' There was only dim light so he was completely confused in the dark. I walked up next to Ramos on his left side, held my Beretta to the lobe of his head, and whispered, "Time's up! That's what's happening!" Then boom! As I was about to turn and make my way back to the front doors, a bodyguard, at least I think he was, staggered out of a small room with an AK hanging off one hand, and a girl flopped on the floor. I dispatched him with two rounds and he fell back into the room. When I checked to see if he was dead, I saw a pile of satchels. I unzipped one and spotted the cash, all bundled in bank wrappers, so I grabbed two satchels!"

S1 started laughing, then shouted down below to Azra saying, "You win the prize, lioness! Expenses reimbursed; you might say!" Azra did not respond. 'D' went below to be with Azra and the kids. Later 'D' explained the money. All Azra said was, "Another five minutes and we could have taken it all!" Then added, "Still, does not come close to compensate for Sharmila or my children!"

Just as daybreak arrived S1 came to a weary team, most sleeping, as best they could during a bumpy ride across the sea to Tortuga Island, and quietly said, "We have the sub on radar folks. We're almost there. Get ready, boys and girls, we're going home! Compliments of the United States Navy!"

On board the sub, as soon as they were settled, Azra spoke with the Captain saying, "There is a message I need to send to my husband." "Come, and we will send it." The captain responded. In the control and communications room of the Boomer, Azra wrote the word and handed it to the sailor at the console. He looked at it, smiled, and then said, "With pleasure mam!" The signal went out: "To Conquest. *"Hallelujah!"*

7

Unfinished Business

The voyage through the Caribbean to the States was not so long. How fast a submerged nuclear submarine travels was not revealed, by anyone. But the team and kids arrived at Kings Bay, on the coast of Georgia, in less than 45 hours. The US Navy Submarine Base was a precious sight for everyone on the team.

An ambulance was waiting to take Sharmila's body to a morgue on the base. Then after being prepared, her body would be air-lifted to her Mozambique home. Before transport, a solemn ceremony was held in a small social activities building near headquarters. In the tradition of the US Navy Seals, each team member stepped forward and slammed their brass shield on top of the coffin of a fallen warrior.

After a superb southern dinner, one last meeting of Team Seven was held at the Hyatt Regency on Jacksonville's waterfront. A private and guarded room was arranged with complimentary fruit and nut baskets, a generous supply of California wines, and champagne, provided by the Navy's Submarine Service.

The president of Dark Fury was there, with his wife, and one of his top mission planners who gave a recap of the mission with video taken by several team members wearing body cams. The report revealed the highest levels of training each member possessed, perfectly applied to a challenging mission.

One additional person was there. A person the team did not know. After all the reporting, shouting, and storytelling was finished, the president introduced her. He stood, saying, "This evening, I have the privilege of introducing a very special person. She has traveled from Washington DC to be with us. In fact, she came from the White House! Ladies and gentlemen, it is an honor to present Ms. Jalena Salisbury, a top aid to the United States President, George H. W. Bush."

Jalena stood, held her linen napkin close to her heart, and said, "It is I who am honored! Honored and privileged to sit and dine with such intrepid warriors, defenders of truth, decency, and freedom. I am especially privileged to be with a woman, two women, to be precise, who are definitely warriors, and, dedicated to life, families, and human rights!"

Picking up two small boxes, she looked at Azra and 'D' saying, "The President has asked me to present, even though it must be done privately, and for good reasons, the Presidential Medal of Freedom to Azra Schaffer and 'D'!" The room exploded with cheers and applause! "And," Jalena added after she could be heard, "It is my privilege to present The Presidential Citation for Valor to Team Seven of Dunkle Wut of Munich, Germany!" Again, the room filled with cheers, whistles, hoots, and applause. So much so, that worried hotel staff attempted to inquire but were turned away by US Marine guards from the base.

Azra and 'D' were invited to speak. They were sitting together and after glancing at each other, one nodded and stood. 'D' spoke first, saying, "This is a great honor for me, a woman from Israel, a caretaker of the Shaffer children." 'D' looked around the room at team members, then said, "Well you are a great bunch of guys and it has been an honor to serve with you on the Caracas mission. I must say though, you really do need to shower more often!" With a smile 'D' sat down among a chorus of hoots and applause.

Azra looked around at the bunch but remained silent for a moment. Then stood, looking squarely at the president of Dark Fury, and said, "Sir, I want to thank you with all my heart for allowing me to join with these excellent men, 'D', and my dear friend Sharmila, to retrieve my children and bring them safely home. I am forever grateful, as is my husband, my mother Adelia, my in-laws, Elsje and Tracey Schaffer, and other team members, known only as Conquest, for what has been accomplished!" A roar and applause hit the ceiling! The Marines joined in.

Jalena left her seat and approached the two women. She embraced them, whispered quiet words, and gave them the medals. After she returned to her seat, she turned to the president. He stood, and she handed him a scroll of parchment tied with a blue ribbon. The president unrolled the scroll, read the citation, and then shook hands with Jalena. Again the room filled with shouts and applause. The official business was concluded. The Marines were invited to indulge in some desserts while three team members replaced them guarding the door.

"There is a matter we need to discuss." Jalena quietly said to Azra and 'D. Azra nodded and the three women went to a corner of the room where they clustered some chairs. After cajoling with a couple of team members, Jalena said, "Our CIA Director has informed us there has been reaction by Bratva and the Russian government which smells like retaliation for the Caracas raid. We have no details but there has been a summons of sorts by Bratva and the KGB to meet at a sight yet to be identified. Some intercepted language and decoded messages suggest the meeting will determine how best to accomplish their objectives in Indonesia and East Africa. And, several key messages included references to Van Steenwijk Shipping and, you Azra. And, I'm sorry to say, your mother, Adelia in Mozambique!"

'D' responded, saying, "I'll contact Mossad and see what they know!"

"Good!" Jalena responded.

Azra was quiet for a moment. Then looked at Jalena and calmly said, "When we were together with Conquest, planning our actions, there were three parts. First, buy time with delay tactics. Second, extract the children, and third, eliminate threats of retaliation by the Russians. We have completed the first two and will engage the third step, the final step, I trust, as soon as possible!" Then added, "We may need your help!"

Jalena looked at Azra, then at 'D' saying, I will convey your plans to the President. I'm certain he would consider a joint operation with Mossad. And, absolutely certain he would have no problem for our people to join with Conquest in the endeavor!"

'D' responded, "At this moment, I cannot speak for Mossad, but when I contact them I'll relay what we know and urge them to assist." Then she added, "As a matter of fact, Mossad has asked me to return as an operations chief. I'm thinking about it."

Azra spoke, saying, "About Conquest, while they are incredible at what they do, and dedicated to the challenges, they are not warriors! We will need to consider protection for them and their families. Since all are American citizens, I would assume such protections will be made available to them."

Jalena instantly responded, "Absolutely! I'll make a note of Conquest, and your concerns, to the President!"

Then, in a most solemn tone, Azra looked squarely at Jalena and added, "As for myself, I will be partnered with 'D'. She and I are a team and, please, tell the President, I have a score to settle on behalf of my father Eka whom Mr. Bush knew years before he was killed by Ivankov and his henchmen. I have sworn to execute that score with the vengeance of my ancestry, gratefulness of posterity, and satisfaction of my heart!"

Jalena was speechless for a few seconds. She nervously swallowed, then said, "My Lord, you are a lioness, just as they described."

'D' smiled and whispered, 'With a terrible vengeance!"

That next day, Dark Fury's president, his wife, and Team Seven, loaded on a private jet and left for Munich. Jalena left in a government jet for Washington D.C. and Azra, and the kids, and 'D,' were flown to Los Alamitos Naval Air Station, near Long Beach, California, aboard a Navy Admirals jet. In a short time after landing, the Schaffer family were nearly reunited. Elsje was scheduled to arrive the next evening from Jakarta. But the celebration began all the same.

The first thing Tommy did was ask 'D' to take him to the bench across the street where they had been abducted. They all went. 'D' asked Tommy, "What is it you are looking for?" Tommy did not answer. He scurried about, looking around the area and under the bench. Then, as he pushed a clump of grass back, he grabbed something, jumped up, and yelled, "My clue I left you my clue!" In his hand was a plastic toy. It was the character *Yoda* from *Star Wars*! Then he said, "I knew Yoda would tell you guys where we were!" "Were you afraid we would not find you?" Azra asked. "No Mom. I'm not afraid, Yoda says, *"Fear is the path to the dark side!"* Bending down a little, Azra asked, "And?" Tommy looked at his mom, then 'D' and soberly said. "I trusted Yoda, and you, Mom, and you 'D'!"

Azra took Tommy in her arms, pressed him close to her, and whispered, "I love you, precious boy!" Teressa took hold of Rowland's hand, Tommy his mom's. Rowland and Azra held hands as they walked, back across Ocean Boulevard to the safety, comfort, and rest of the Schaffer home.

After Elsje had rested from her traveling home from Jakarta, the family, Tracey, Elsje, Rowland, and Azra, and the kids, along with 'D', decided to take Fair Wind for a sail down the coast to Newport Beach and back. At Newport Beach, they entered the harbor and had a lovely tour around the bay and Balboa Island. At one point Tracey showed the kids where John Wayne lived. Tommy was in absolute awe.

On the sail back, they entered Alamitos Bay and motored about with Elsje and Tracey acting as tour guides, pointing out the lovely homes of Naples Island and the famous racing yachts that sail to Honolulu and Tahiti. It was while visiting Alamitos Bay that a call came from Mossad on the satellite phone asking for 'D'. Going forward to the bow, she talked for a few minutes then returned to the cockpit, looked at Tracey and Rowland, and said, "Mossad and your Navy Seals have formed a pact to jointly engage in Operation Intervention"!

Rowland clapped his hands and Azra smiled, saying, "And with Conquest, we have a super-team, a team that will not fail!" Tracey quickly commented, "When we get home today, I think it would be well to contact and gather the Conquest team together as soon as possible. We need to get into those Russians' living room. We need to know precisely what they are doing, when, and how!"

Rowland responded, "Will do, dad. I'll get hold of Pong and he can get the word out." Azra spoke, saying, "I do not believe we'll have a problem getting the girls to come."

"Great!" Elsje said. Then Tracey added, "The study and library will do as the 'war room' but we'll need to figure out what to do for sleeping arrangements."

"Girls inside and boys outside! That's the rule!" Teressa shouted.

"Hey, that's a great idea!" Rowland responded. Looking at Tracey, he added, "We could rent an RV and billet them comfortably. All we need to do is fit the thing in that huge garage we have!"

Tracey gave a curious look at Elsje who smiled. Then Elsje leaned toward Teressa and whispered, "Girls inside, boys outside? Whose rule is that?" Teressa whispered back, "I just thought it up." They did a hand slap-n-shake then laughed together.

Tracey steered Fair Wind for the Long Beach Marina. Just as the sun was setting the sky turned a mellow amber. It had been a beautiful, balmy mid-April day. A day of recovery, both body and spirit. A day of refreshing for a family strained near the breaking point by evil forces.

Three days later, a start date for planning Operation Intervention was set. Conquest, with every member of the team committed, was activating. "The first order of business when they get here is to establish a secure communication system with our Navy Seals and Mossad!" Rowland announced.

"No need to wait!" Tracey said. I'll make a call."

Four days passed before Pongo, Pac-Man, Elite, Fawcett and Pankhurst had all arrived. The boys were bunked in an Airstream RV which barely squeezed into the four-car garage with a storage loft. The girls were put in the spare guest room Codi and Elam had occupied. Codi and Elam were back with their unit in Arizona but kept in the communication loop.

After some minor kinks, the U.S. Navy established clear working procedures and protocols with Mossad. A secure communication network was set up and was fully operational. Real-time information flowed between the three players. With additional intelligence gathering by the CIA, all were working as one in discovering where, and when, the anticipated Bratva and Russian KGB meeting would occur. And, who would be there? But the pipeline went dark. The Russians were saying nothing, not to anyone.

"It's been a week Tracey! Nothing substantial has been revealed. Just more of the same chatter about this grand meeting those devils are going to have!" Elsje was frustrated. Almost everyone was. It was late, very late. Elsje had just taken snacks and fresh water to the Conquest team who had been laboring on phones and computers for ten hours. Exhaustion was becoming evident. Exhaustion? Or was it frustration causing a cloud of disappointment? Whatever! The team was becoming testy!

Suddenly the house phone rang. Tracey answered, saying, "Schaffer residence!" Then his face lit up shouting, "Adelia, I can barely hear you! Are you okay?" Azra, upon hearing Tracey's voice, came running. Tracey handed the phone to Azra saying, "I'll put her on speaker. Think we can hear better!" Azra shook her head in agreement and said, "Mother! Wonderful to hear your voice."

"Well dearest, there has been a lot of celebration since we learned of the children being recovered and that you are safe. Lots of celebration!" Adelia was near shouting.

Here as well mother, here as well!" Azra responded.

Several of the Conquest team left their computers and phones and came to the library, listening to Adelia, whose voice was much more distinct on speaker. Rowland offered his love and asked, "What's happening? How is the fishing and canning?"

"Oh the fishing has been wonderful and each cannery is operating at full capacity. We have received more orders from African countries and as far east as Australia and New Zealand. All seems well at the moment!" Adelia gleefully said. Then added, "Actually, I called to relate something that happened that I am certain may help. Is the team there?" A chorus answered, 'Yes, we are here!" Adelia laughed, saying, "Wish I could be with you wonderful people!"

Azra then asked, "What is it, mother? What happened?"

"Okay, the other day, two men were caught taking photographs of the ships, canneries, our lories, warehouses, and even my residence. Our security people took the men to a room near the Maputo office to interrogate them and discovered after they finally spoke, that they were Russian citizens. But they would not say more!"

The team looked at each other in anticipation, then excitedly focused again on the speaker and what Adelia was saying or about to say.

"Are the children still up?" Adelia asked. "No, Mother, they are asleep. It is after midnight here, about nine hours behind your time." Azra responded. Adelia then said, "Good! What I have to say is not for tender ears!"

"Well, Hamza, chief of security, you know, father's boyhood friend, was tired of the games these Russians were playing so suggested another game, a dare-game really, one he and your dad would play when boys. It was leaping over snake pits! So they cleared all the stuff out of the Lorie Repair Shop pit, you know, the trench where they get under the lorry and work on them, then tossed in a few Puff Adders and Cobras. Then rigged the electric hoist with a chair, stripped one of the Russians to his *"Fruit of the Looms"*, tied him in, then maneuvered the hoist over the pit, inching the Russian down while asking, who he was, why he was there, who he worked for, what he was planning to do with all the photos, and anything else he wished to say before his feet came within striking distance of some very angry and energized snakes!"

Fawcett gasped. Pankhurst shuddered! Elite muttered, "Holy Moley!"

Adelia continued, saying, "Well, from what they told me, the hoist jerked a little. The Russian slipped out of the chair bindings just enough that his legs were thrashing about, barely above the adders. But two huge cobras struck and the Russian screamed. But instead of pressing the up button, Hedy, who was operating the hoist, was so excited, I guess, he pressed the down button, and the Russian was instantly attacked by all the snakes!"

"What did the other Russian do or say when that happened?" Rowland asked.

Hamza told me that, "He screamed. Even being all tied up, he flopped about on the floor like a floundering shark. Then Hamza told me they pulled his friend up out of the pit and laid him on the floor where he went into convulsions and died. Then Abilio, who was helping, set the same chair down in front of the blubbering Russian, pulled him into the chair, and began wrapping the line around him. The Russian screamed he would tell all, saying, "Just don't set me down in that snake pit!"

"What did he say?" 'D' asked.

"Oh 'D'! I recognize your voice! How are you?" Adelia shouted. "I am well madam, well enough!" 'D' responded.

"So, sorry for the long story, but here is what was said! Bratva and Russian KGB are going to hold a meeting with several Russian army and navy officers, and other people, from Uzbeki, Ukraine, Turkman, Belarus, Moldavia, and other places, to plan a takeover of several companies including Van Steenwijk Shipping and our fishing and canning business. They will hold the meeting on a gigantic yacht called *"SHADOW"* owned by a Russian billionaire. His name is Roman Fukin!

"Where and when is the meeting?" Azra asked.

"I have it written here. The location is Antaly harbor. It is in Turkey on the south coast at the east end of the Mediterranean. The date is June 7th. The Russian also said there was a huge party planned aboard before the meeting was to start. They seem to want to pay favors to friends and celebrate victories before the fact of outcomes!"

"What did you do with the Russian?" Pankhurst asked.

Adelia responded, "I assume you're with my daughter for I do not recognize your voice. However, he is dead as well. We took him to the old prison here in Maputo and he swallowed a poison pill just as they got him in a cell." Adelia responded. Then added, "They die very hard! Indeed, they die hard, those Russians!"

"How many will be on the yacht?" Tracey asked.

"Not certain. The Russian only guessed about that question, saying maybe eighty, or more! Likely included the girls they rent! One other thing, now this is a treasure: Ivankov, Dima, Alexander, Alexi and Sergi, and Viktor, along with a woman by the name of Anya Kisselyov, she's with Bratva as well, will definitely be there!" Adelia excitedly said. Then she added, "And, all the pictures they took have been destroyed!"

Suddenly, the transmission became fuzzy. In a last effort to hear, all that could be heard was, "Love to my children!" The call ended.

After a few seconds of stunned silence, The whole Conquest crew cheered and hooted! Rowland jumped to a computer and began an encrypted message to the CIA and Navy liaison officer coordinating intelligence for the Seals assigned to the operation. Pac-Man jumped to his computer and accessed military satellite imagery with coding to locate the Russian Yacht, *SHADOW*. After a few moments, he shouted, "Holy cow! That monster yacht is 553 feet long and has four deck levels above the main deck. It also has top security systems, video, motion, etc. That's the biggest yacht I have ever seen." The whole Conquest team crowded around the computer screen and stared in silence.

'D' called her contact, Matthew, at Mossad in Tele Aviv and relayed information from notes taken while Adelia was talking. After days and nights, of frustration, data began spilling into the information coffers of three or four agencies, in the United States and Israel. All due, actually, because of a dare game Eka and his friend played when they were kids in Mozambique. Jumping over a snake pit!

Hovering over a computer and several monitors, Elite and Pong were talking about strategies for hacking *SHADOW's* security systems. "Okay, okay, I get it. But let's give them something totally different, totally weird, man, really weird!" Pong shouted!

"What's happening, guys?" Rowland asked.

Pong turned, smiled, and said, "Genius here just hacked into SHADOW's security and we're haggling over a cover image to plaster all over their screens from top to bottom of that floating stinkpot!"

"I've got it!" Elite shouted. With a cheesy cat smile he spun around in his swivel chair and pointed at the screen. A huge image of Kong was jumping around beating on his chest. "You want audio?" Elite said as he swung back to the console. He typed in a few commands and pushed back just as Kong, jumping and pounding about, began doing gorilla grunts! "You want faster?" Again, Elite went to his keyboard, pushed a few keys, then swung back. In all its weirdest glory, the screen filled with a gorilla on steroids, grunting, puffing, and growling! "You want action?" Elite shouted. Another few commands and he had Kong jumping, puffing, growling, and tossing grenades. Each grenade appeared to fly toward a viewer watching any screen, then explode in rapid succession.

"Alright!" Rowland and Pong shouted. The three of them slapped their hands in high-five fashion. Then Rowland said, "Get it ready for insertion! But not until we are set!" Elite saluted saying, "Aye, aye, Commander Kong.

Azra, watching Kong and the guys, began laughing. Then, gaining composure, said, "Between what we now have, and what the U.S. Navy, Mossad, and CIA have, we will need to get the plan organized."

'D' responded, "Mossad wants the strategy work done live and eye to eye. We cannot risk leaking any aspect of what we are about to attempt." "Same for our contact with the Navy," Fawcett added. Tracey commented he would find out what venue the Navy and CIA wanted to use for the session, adding, "You know, organizing a plan may require several days." All agreed there was a ton of work to do and little time left to do it!

The Pentagon was instantly ruled out. "Leaks like a sieve!" The Navy liaison officer commented. CIA headquarters was a possibility but was in overload due to the Gulf War and other international matters, including a push by the Chinese to establish a stronger presence in the South China Sea. After some back and forth, an aide to President Bush said the president was willing to offer his home at the Bush Compound located at Kennebunkport, Main. She added, "The First Lady says, so long as you stay out of the kitchen!"

There was considerable discussion but all agreed it would be the most suitable place. The president's secret service detail, with other security protections, and the fact the place was typically known for family and social events, would not generate suspicions. Also, it was located outside the Washington DC gaggle of reporters and media hounds.

The only drawback, if there was any, was those attending would need to come with the intelligence they had. And, be able to communicate changes or updates when necessary. Perhaps it was not the best location, but after all the maybes and options were considered, The Bush Compound was selected! Rowland, Azra, and 'D' would represent Conquest. Matthew and another Mossad agent would fly from Tele Aviv. The Navy was sending three of its top people and the CIA, one of their chief agents.

In the government van, taking Rowland and Azra, and 'D' from the airport to the compound, Azra commented, "It's May 2nd!" 'D' muttered back, "Yes, and there is little time to get this organized. We must be operational and all assets in place at least two days before the June 7th meeting!" "The timing for shutting down their eyes and ears is critical. But I have to believe each player knows that." Rowland commented.

"I'm confident they do!" 'D' responded. Then added, "The larger question is infiltration. Who and how will we get people on that yacht to set the whole thing in motion? And get our own eyes and ears on target?"

"I've been thinking about that. You and I, 'D', are going to join the party!" Azra quietly said. She was not smiling. 'D' was silent, as was Rowland, for a moment. Then 'D' slowly smiled, saying, "That just may work!" Rowland finally got beyond the stupor that had hold of him, saying, "Are you two crazy? How would you ever get past their security? How would you exit? How would you..."

"We'll join the party girls!" Azra interrupted. Adding, "And I know just the person who can arrange it!"

"You do?" Rowland was becoming completely undone. He tried to say more but stuttered, something he rarely did except when excited, or dumbfounded! It was a carry-over from childhood. A mild case of dyslexia.

Azra assured Rowland there was nothing to worry about, except the mission. Then she explained she and her friends had met a girl at Oxford who was working on a master's in economics but definitely lived on the wild side of life to pay for her education. "She, if anyone, will know about what was happening aboard the yacht *SHADOW*!" Azra quietly said.

Then and there, Azra called Fawcett and related a contact request. Fawcett laughed as she responded, "Will do! You are really crazy, but my pleasure!" Not more than ten minutes passed. They were just about to arrive at the Bush Compound when Azra's phone pinged. The person calling was shouting, laughing, giggling, then said, "So you want to play? Wow, girl, I never would have guessed!" Azra responded, "Hello Marlene, how's life treating you?" Marlene responded, "Oh somewhere around 700k annually, tax-free! And, I'm feeling great! Then she asked, 'Where are you?"

Rowland rolled his eyes. Azra then said, "Cannot tell where I am. But have a question. Do you know of a high-class party in the Mediterranean happening around the first week in June on a Russian yacht?"

Marlene responded, "Do I? Hell yes girl, it's a Russian gig and I do mean gig with a capital 'G'! It's on some billionaire's yacht. They're soliciting top escorts and call girls for the show out of England, France, Germany, Belgium, and just about anywhere they can find them. Some European rock band is going to be there, and a bunch of European rich guys wanting to have fun!"

"You going?" Azra asked. "Would not miss this one!" Marlene responded. Then asked, "Why, you serious? Do you want in? If you do it will be a four-day stint so bring a resuscitator. Why, girl, you blow me away. You're not doing this for frolic, or mula, are you? So, what's up?"

"No, not fun or frolic! I have an old score to settle!" Azra flatly said.

"Oh, juicy! Love it! Who's the creep?" Marlene snapped back.

Azra laughed, saying, "You would not know him. I cannot tell you. If I did, I'd have to kill you!"

"In that case, keep it to yourself," Marlene responded. Then said, "But if you really, really, really want, or need, to go, I'll get you a ticket!"

"It would be two tickets!" Azra responded.

"Two!" Marlene shouted. "Even better! Hot doggies! Anyone from Oxford?"

"I'll let you know in a day or so, maybe sooner! Azra said. Then quickly added, "Got to go! Don't talk about this with anyone and I mean anyone! Okay?"

"Not even my kitty Marty?" Marlene shouted.

"Especially your kitty Marty!" Azra said. They both laughed and closed the call.

They were at the gate. The van driver told them they would need to exit the vehicle. On getting out, Rowland whispered, "Good grief sweetheart! Do you think that's a good idea? I mean, will it actually work?"

"Not certain yet, husband. Let's see how this goes with the others." Azra quietly responded. Then she stopped and turned to Rowland, looked solemnly into his eyes, and said, "There is unfinished business that must be completed. And by the soul of my dead father, I'm going to finish it."

An instant later Secret Service agents greeted them. Two well-dressed men and a beautiful girl who looked young enough to be someone's teenage daughter. The three agents kindly introduced themselves and then asked for identification. After checks were made, the more senior agent smiled and said, "Welcome to the Bush Family home."

8

Righteous Resolve

The amassed strategic thinking capacity of people gathered in a special room for planning Operation Intervention was incredible. Nearly instantaneous support assets accelerated the organization of the plan. Within six hours, the basic framework was set. Details and option scenarios were now on the table for discussion. Commander Paul Wiggins, U.S. Navy Seals, was elected to lead the group.

Commander Wiggins stood and went to a large video screen. With a swagger in hand, he addressed the group, saying, "So, we have established the target is Bratva leadership and collateral adversaries actively engaged in deception and terrorism activity in Indonesia and East African countries! The venue is the private vessel Shadow located, or will be located, in the harbor of Antalya, Turkey."

"The assault plan has three elements, infiltration, takedown, and destruction. Operational control will be with Seal Team Eight in coordination with Mossad Secret Service. And, infiltration of two women from Conquest who have specific targets assigned. Targeting for land and vessel-positioned sniper teams will be directed by Navy Seal Team Eight under the command of Master Chief Petty Officer Larry

Panel. Chief Panel will recite the details we have so far established."

With that introduction, Master Chief Petty Officer Panel rose and was offered the swagger by Commander Wiggins. He approached the video screen and pointed to a visual that zeroed in on Odessa, providing satellite details. "Here is where the Shadow is berthed at present." A murmur trailed around the room over the size of the yacht. "Based on access to a float plan for the vessel confirmed two days ago by Mossad, in five days she will sail through the Black Sea to Istanbul where she will berth, load supplies, and board additional crew, servants, party girls, and some officials as well as entertainers." The imagery spotted the precise location Shadow would be berthed, with details of surroundings.

Chief Panel continued, "After the loading and boarding is complete, which is estimated to take two days, Shadow will sail through the Sea of Marmara and into the Dardanelles Straight. Then into and through the Aegean Sea to Antalya and anchor just outside Roman Harbor, on the west side, where the sea floor is deep enough to accommodate the vessel. She will be at anchor by the afternoon of June 5th."

The imagery focused on vessels that were there, buildings that surrounded the harbor edge, and the piers enclosing the harbor. The Chief pointed to the buildings saying, "Our task is to suppress and dispatch Bratva guards, and, execute underwater demolition. Seal snipers and spotters will position around Shadow. One team on this building, another on this pier, and a third sniper team will be camouflaged on a floating platform off the bow of where Shadow is anchored." Then he added, "On command, the rest of the team will be executing a submerged attack, setting twelve shape charges critical at points along the haul for remote detonation to destroy the vessel. Their extraction will be via surface craft after distancing Shadow by one mile underwater. They then will transfer to a submarine stationed offshore about four miles."

The Chief looked about the room and said, "Each of us, Seals, Mossad, and Conquest have code names for our people. Unless otherwise required or suggested, it is best we retain those names and not use actual names, before, during, or immediately after the operation. However, command and control will be the responsibility of Commander Wiggins. Now, memorize his code name, and please, do not write it down! The code is Gaza-1. When you hear Gaza-1, know that a legitimate command is being given. As deployment and operations begin I will manage on-target logistics. My code is Gaza-2!" He glanced at Azra and smiled. She nodded an acknowledgment.

Chief Panel then pointed to Matthew from Mossad and said, "Sir, your turn!" Matthew stood and said, "Israel, and many others around the world, have been plagued far too long by this band of malicious goats. Our agents, along with one CIA agent, who is boarding at Odessa, will board Shadow at Istanbul. There will be six Mossad, posing as galley servants and general cleaning and maintenance crew. Weapons, clothing, and gear, including night vision and communications headsets, will be boarded in frozen containers marked "Chicken Breasts", in Turkish, with three Red Stars painted with reflective paint at the edge of each container." Then, looking at 'D' and Azra, he said, "Another container marked "Red Wheat Flour", also in Turkish, with three red stars painted on the edge, will contain weapons, clothing, and gear for the ladies." Everyone glanced at 'D' and Azra, nodding their support.

Then Matthew added, "Mossad agents have the privilege of dispatching key Bratva leaders. Here are their faces." Matthew turned to the screen where a set of images appeared. "First, Lev Morozoy! Head of Bratva and very tight with the Kremlin. Second, Ivankov, a unit leader with charge over Indonesia and East Africa. Third, his bodyguard, Dima, is a ruthless killer. Fourth, Alexander tortures and has no human feelings. Next, is Alexi, who is smart, witty, and handsome, but also a killer. Then Sergi who is an expert at explosives and demolition. Next, Viktor is one of the most skillful assassins on the planet! Then we have a new player, a woman known as Anya Kisselyov. She is a master at baiting men to their deaths by poison or needles. And I do not mean acupuncture!"

Matthew continued, saying, "Allow me to make clear, the only one of these we will attempt to take alive is Lev, the head of Bratva. If we cannot, he will be dispatched. The other, who is assigned to our ladies here from Conquest, is Ivankov. Ivankov will be taken by Azra or 'D' or both, in whatever manner and whatever timing they devise on site!"

After a pause, Matthew continued, saying, "Our extraction assets consist of two helicopters staged on Cypress at a British RAF base located at Akrotiri. On advance signal, our Super-Cobra gunship will fly to the site and be on target providing suppressing fire. At 220 miles per hour, flight time is estimated to be one hour. When clear, a Black Hawk will land on Shadow's heliport and extract our people, including 'D' and Azra. Timing is critical!

Turning to 'D' Matthew bowed, slightly, then smiled, saying, "Your turn, ladies!"

'D' spoke from where she sat. "Azra and I will be boarding at Istanbul with 23 other women. They are, as the world calls them, Escorts, or call girls, which is a watered way of labeling highly paid prostitutes. As referenced, our primary objective is to eliminate Ivankov, then aid Mossad in their assignment in whatever manner required."

Another member of the Navy Seals, an assistant to Commander Wiggins, said, "So, let's be clear, you are executing your task as a matter of personal satisfaction?" Azra looked squarely at the man and said, "Not just personal, sir, *extremely* personal!" Then added, "If you or anyone has an issue, please state it now!" Azra looked around the table. None said a word. Then Commander Wiggins, calmly stated, "Everyone here sustains your objective Mrs. Schaffer, and fully appreciate your capacity to carry it out!" As others nodded and muttered agreement, Commander Wiggins gave a sharp glance at his assistant who immediately retracted his comment, saying, "I apologize madam. I read the reports on the Caracas raid and now I am fully convinced. I support your service on this mission."

"So!" Commander Wiggins said, "Now we have a mysterious side of the operation, the Conquest team represented by Mr. Rowland Schaffer. Your turn, sir!

Rowland stood, Looked about the room, and said, "We have already hacked into Bratva and the vessel Shadow. Our 'mysterious' team of boys and girls are paired with CIA surveillance systems. In fact, we are prepared to shut Shadow down! Their lights, security systems, and communications, electronically, for about 45 minutes. Beyond that if possible. And, we will have real-time imagery of all exterior actions visible by satellite. That imagery will be available to all teams operating on or off the vessel!"

Rowland continued, "Our imaging systems will also transmit interior action via body cameras. Those who will be wearing the devices are yours, Mossad, to select. So, we suggest the actionable time on target be no more than 30 minutes. And, extraction is complete in no more than 40 minutes from the moment an executed order is released by Gaza-1. When the extraction is complete, and personnel are clear of Shadow's blast zone, the command for detonation will be given by Gaza-1." As he sat, Rowland glanced at Azra. His glance was met with a slim smile.

Commander Wiggins leaned forward in his chair, saying, "Gentlemen, and ladies, the command to execute action for the mission is "TULIP"! Now, let's ferret out details and submit this plan for a Rabbinical Seal of approval!" Matthew and his assistant smiled and nodded. Others joined in applause and then, looking at Azra and 'D,' applauded louder. 'D' and Azra joined as well!

Just then, two secret service agents entered the room. One said, Please excuse the interruption, The President would appreciate a word with you!" In walked President George H.W. Bush. Everyone stood.

"Please, relax folks, I know you're involved in a vital mission and just wanted to stop by and offer my most sincere wishes for success. And, it would be our pleasure, Barbra and I, to host you for dinner this evening at 8:00." There was a round of thank you's, verbal and nodding. Then President Bush smiled, waved, and left.

The group bore down on details the rest of the day. It was nearly 6:30 in the evening when Commander Wiggins suggested they break, freshen, and prepare to attend the dinner. All readily agreed.

The dinner was delightful. President Bush and the First Lady, Barbra, asked no questions about the mission, and no comments were offered. But there was talk of the Caracas mission with Dark Fury and the recovery of Teressa and Tommy. President Bush expressed high regard for the necessary work of Dark Fury in the Middle East, Europe, and Africa. Then he focused on 'D', Azra, and Rowland, with numerous recalls of times past when he and Barbra visited the Van Steenwijk home in Jakarta and the fishing and canning facilities at Maputo. It was a time when Eka was yet alive and very active, along with Adelia, helping restore Mozambique's civility and commerce during and after the devastating civil wars.

By the end of the next day, a mission statement and operations plan for Operation Intervention was complete. It needed endorsement and approval by certain military and civilian leaders of both Israel and the United States. And, it was agreed, to advise Interpol and Dutch Security Services as to essential elements of the plan and request they be prepared to assist if needed in Turkey and elsewhere.

In separate small groups, over the next 24 hours, the mission planners departed The Bush Compound. Matthew and his aide returned to Tele Aviv. The Navy officers returned to their headquarters.

'D', Azra and Rowland returned to Long Beach, California where they were greeted by Tracey, Elsje, Sophia, and Isabella, two younger sisters of Rowland having returned, Sophia from Jakarta, Isabella from MIT, and her university studies.

Teressa and Tommy could not wait to hug their parents, and 'D'. Having been under the strict guardianship of their grandparents, Tracey and Elsje, they complained, but just a little. The Conquest team stayed in the study at their consoles and phones, working through new information rapidly flowing through the pipeline.

Consuelo and Priscilla, along with Sophia and Isabella, and Elsje, put together a superb meal to celebrate their being together after a very long time being apart. Prime rib with all the trimmings and side dishes anyone could devise, in the Shaffer's huge kitchen, was gently prepared and respectfully enjoyed. The dinner was followed by a gathering of storytelling and songs. Isabella was an accomplished pianist and her older sister, Sophia, was a trained soprano vocalist. There was no space for sorrow. No moments of worries. It was simply a family, and true friends, relishing an evening in the safety and peace of home. Tracey was the first to fall asleep.

After Tommy and Terresa were put in their beds, Rowland, Azra, and 'D' joined with Pong, Pac Man and Elite, and Fawcett and Pankhurst, and held a briefing. There were more details to consider, details that held the potential for complicating the mission.

Pointing to the latest satellite images, Pac-Man led the conversation, saying, "The helipad on Shadow is stationed with a 'Kacatka', a Kamov-60, high-speed helicopter. It would have to be removed or destroyed. Also, there are three pontoon surface vessels each carrying two of Shadow's security personnel, heavily armed. They appear deployed and circling Shadow, or at station points, whenever Shadow is moored or at anchor." And, Pac Man continued, pointing to a small and barely visible detail, "Look at this! Shadow is fitted with anti-aircraft missiles. If they are able to fire those babies, POOF! The Cobra, and perhaps black hawk, go down!"

'D' took a close look at the images. She turned to Rowland saying, 'As for the missile launchers, I and another Mossad agent can disable them. As for the bums in those pontoon boats, Seal snipers can take them out when the party begins!" "What about the helicopter?" Rowland asked. 'D' thought a second then said, "We will need to get one of our Mossad agents who can fly the thing. We'll need him, or her, on board to fly it off. Far too dangerous trying to destroy it with rockets off a Cobra. No telling what damage may occur to the pad. And, the wreckage may stay in place, preventing the extraction helicopter from safely landing."

The work continued into the early morning hours. Finally, Conquest needed sleep. Each member found their way to the rooms or the RV. It had been a good day, a long day, a day which allowed detailed raking through the mission. What was discovered was transmitted to the CIA, Navy, and Tele Aviv. Still, Rowland and Azra quietly chatted, tossing various scenarios about, searching for options. The option Rowland searched for hardest was one where Azra was not aboard the Russian yacht! Such an option never matured.

"Operation Intervention approved!" Was the encrypted message from Navy Seals headquarters. "It's a go!" Pongo shouted. A few moments later another message came saying that the Insertion of Mossad at Istanbul was to be June 1st. On-site positioning at Antalya compete June 4th, and execution is set for June 7th, at 2240 hrs. Extraction set at 2310 hours Team Timing devices for charges set on command, with detonation estimated at 2330 hrs."

Each member of the team, be they Conquest, Seals, or Mossad, had code names. Azra and 'D' retained theirs from the Caracas raid. Arrangements for transporting weapons, ammunition, gear, and clothing in specially marked containers had been made. Two Mossad agents were to board Shadow at Odessa. One was a woman, with helicopter pilot expertise flying Russian helicopters. She would work in Shadow's galley. The other, a man, would serve as a waiter and card dealer in the lavish game and entertainment room built into the lower decks of the vessel.

Four additional Mossad agents, along with Azra and 'D', who would be with Marlene and the escorts, would board in Istanbul. Each having been vetted by the KGB. The CIA created profiles for Azra, and 'D' which placed them near the top-paid professional escorts known in England or Europe. 'D' studied her phony profile and whispered to Azra, "Thinking about a career change?" They chuckled a little then simultaneously said, "Na, way too old!"

The tension was far too apparent as 'D' and Azra departed. LAX was crowded. As it always is. Rowland, with Teressa and Tommy, clung to their mother for a few moments outside the Turkish Airlines boarding area. All waiting for the call to board the Red Eye to Istanbul but resisting it happening. Tommy cried but Teressa held back, trying to be the grown-up she wanted desperately to become. Rowland, who loved Azra dearly, held his emotions as best he could; yet, was powerless to stop his eyes from watering.

The boarding call came. Last hugs all around! Then one last kiss with the whisper, "God go with you!" from Rowland, then a shout, "With you both!" With a wave and another kiss blown by Azra to her children, the two women disappeared down the covered ramp.

After being seated in first class, attendants stuffing their carry-bags in the bin above, Azra looked out the window, trying to catch a glimpse of Rowland and the kids. Nothing! Finally, she leaned back whispering, "I know we must do this, but if there were any other way, I'd gladly take it." 'D' said nothing. Just handed Azra a tissue to catch a small tear sliding off the edge of her eye. Then pulled a magazine out of the seat-pouch leaned back, and quietly said, "We are going to send them to hell, L3! And hell is anxious to have them!"

Azra smiled and responded, "Right you are, K2...right you are! Straight to hell!"

The flight was long. Very long. But the taxi ride to the Four Seasons Hotel at the Bosporus, where they would gather with other escort girls for a couple of nights, was short, about thirty minutes short. In the large ornate foyer, they spotted Marlene. She was easy to spot. Tall, 5 foot and 9 inches tall, with long flaming red hair, and a shape that, on-site, caused men to fall to their knees. And, her British accent and laughter bounced off marble columns as she chatted with three men, all young Turks.

"Seen any Oxford grads wandering about?" Azra whispered from behind Marlene. Marlene swirled around, grabbed Azra, and squealed delight at their reunion. 'D' stepped forward and extended a hand. Marlene did not take it. Instead, she grabbed 'D' in the same manner and hugged her saying, "Such a delight that you can join us for this party!" As she was hugging, she whispered, "Hug me darling, we're being watched." 'D' quickly returned the hug and smiled broadly.

"Well, ladies, let's check in!" Marlene muttered. The three Turks quickly offered to handle their Italia-Retro roller suitcases and carry-ons." The women consented. As Azra was offering her carry-on bag to one of the fellows, she glanced toward a couch where a very Russian-looking fellow sat holding a newspaper, was staring at them.

Marlene leaned over, feigning a tug at her shirt, and whispered, "They're all over the place. Welcoming committee and head counters. Not dangerous. I hope!" Then laughing, she did a sexy walk toward the reception desk where two attendants stood, obviously anxious to serve. Azra and 'D' followed suit, trying their best to mimic models walking down a New York fashion runway. After such a long flight, it was a mite challenging but redeeming exercise!

No sooner had they entered their rooms, which were connected, than Marlene went to Azra's room and knocked. Azra asked who it was and Marlene responded, "Your favorite playgirl! Who else?" Then laughed. Azra opened the door and pulled Marlene inside. As she did Azra glanced both directions down the hallway. No one was seen.

While shutting and locking the door, Marlene said, "Okay girl. I know something serious is happening or you and your friend would not be here!" Azra didn't say a word. Instead, she went to the connecting room door and knocked. 'D' opened the door and stepped in with a finger to her lips signaling silence. Azra went to a stereo unit and turned on rather rambunctious Turkish music. Then the three women huddled around a crystal-topped coffee table.

Whispering just loud enough for Marlene to hear, 'D' said, "Look, Marlene, You are here for the party but we're here to bust that party. By that I mean there will be people who will not walk away! It is an international effort to rid our planet of malicious evil and Russian designs on subjugating millions of people. You have been a great help getting Azra and me here, but you must understand that from here on, you will need to be careful, especially when around us, or you could, well, end up very dead."

Marlene's face went to chalk as she looked at Azra, then back at 'D', then said, "I don't wish to get in anyone's way. I think I understand what you are doing, but, I can handle myself pretty well, and, well, I may be able to help!"

'D' looked at Azra who nodded understanding. But then Azra looked at Marlene and said, "For all intent and purpose, 'D' is a Mossad agent. I represent another group and we are paired with US Navy Seals and Mossad agents to carry out a very dangerous mission!"

"What mission?" Marlene asked.

'D' whispered. "We're going to blow that yacht and everyone on it to kingdom come!" Then added, "After Azra and I make sure certain Russian thugs are eliminated!"

Marlene jerked back. Her beautiful face, again, turned white. She shuddered a little and wrapped her arms around herself as if caught in a sudden chill. Then, bent over and silently stared at the floor, her long silky red hair falling lazily to her knees.

Azra reached out and placed her hand on Marlene's shoulder. Then whispered, "Do not worry, we will take you with us when the work is done."

Marlene looked at Azra for a moment. She straightened her posture, then smiled, saying, "Good Lord, I'd sure hope so!"

The three women continued talking for some time. It was agreed that Marlene should stay observant, offer warnings or advice, as appropriate, but not try and engage in any way when taking down bad men, and women. Marlene, while lacking in the levels of training 'D' and Azra possessed, had sufficient to at least protect herself. Though a tall beautiful, slim woman, and a very popular escort, she was no prissy missy!

Additional women arrived. It became quite noticeable in the lavish dining room at the hotel that evening. Clusters of beautiful women were seated at numerous tables, chatting in multiple languages with no consideration of volume! Marlene fluently spoke five languages. 'D', five as well, and Azra about seven, including Chinese and Russian.

The next day, about mid-morning, the phone rang in Azra's room, then 'D's. In fact, it rang in all rooms where escorts, gathered for the grand party, were doing their best to overcome jet lag and a late night.

All were summoned to a large conference room at the east end of the hotel on the mezzanine level. They were to be there at noon sharp where lunch, or brunch, if preferred, would be served.

When Azra and 'D' arrived, they discovered something more was being served. A heavy dose of indoctrination and rules of the road. On a large video screen were images of the yacht, details of staterooms, where the women would be berthed. They were shown the dining room, casino, entertainment venues, cocktail lounges, and other places within the yacht's several deck levels. Places where they could go, and places where they absolutely could not. When the Russian woman giving the lecture, who spoke in English, introduced herself as "Anya", Azra nudged 'D". 'D' slowly nodded in recognition of the name. It was the woman working with Bratva, Anya Kisselyov, the assassin!

The CIA profile for Azra had her named "Lily Tennison". 'D' was named Marlo Casey. The fake profiles worked. No one raised an eyebrow. No one, that is, except Anya who appeared suspicious of everyone and everything.

At the luncheon, Anya sat near Azra, not next to her but across the round dining table. As they were eating, Anya looked at Azra and casually said, "Lily! To be certain a lovely name. And most certainly, you are a beautiful woman. There is a man I know and work with who, I am confident, would be delighted with your company!"

In Russian, Azra responded, "Oh, who might this gentleman be?" Anya looked at Azra a second, smiled, and said, also in Russian, "He is known as Ivankov, a handsome and strong man, and highly respected of the Kremlin…and a high-ranking officer of Bratva!" Then added, "He is especially fond of black women!" Others at the table giggled.

"Bratva? What is Bratva?" Azra asked. Her eyes pretended curiosity.

Anya staged a wry smile, saying, "An outstanding benevolent society." Adding, "Bratva has been around a very long time and has friends everywhere, even Africa!

Before the meeting ended, the women were instructed to be in front of the hotel by 10:00 am the following morning, wearing their digital wrist passes to be scanned. There would be a bus to take them to the yacht Shadow for boarding where they would be scanned again and searched.

When back in their rooms, Azra, 'D', and Marlene gathered together in Azra's room. With the music turned up, they talked over some, not all, details regarding what was about to happen once the vessel was anchored at Antalya. Marlene listened intently. After 'D' was finished, Marlene said, "I'm all in ladies. I have every hope that your mission will be successful. While these people mean commerce to me, and others, in truth, they are scum, and we, meaning we women who live secret lives, all know it! Trust me, I'll do what I can!"

The next morning, twenty-three *tarnished angels*, plus two women, empowered with righteous resolve, dedicated to destroying a nest of evil plaguing them for over a decade, boarded a luxury tour bus. In a short time, they came to the main Istanbul Ferry Terminal. Not more than a hundred yards just beyond the terminal, at a long quay, the Russian Yacht Shadow sat, bristling with heavily armed guards!

'D' and Azra took a careful look. They scanned every foot of every level, picking out details and storing them in their minds. They would need that information in a few days when they, and their fellow warriors, would receive the command to attack.

Azra quietly commented, "I count twelve guards." 'D' responded, "Thirteen, actually, one just showed up on the bow. But that's just this side of the boat! If equally dispersed, there must be at least twenty-six! Perhaps more below or in reserve!" Azura looked again, spotted the guard, then said, "Most carry AK's." 'D' whispered back, "There are two with 9A's, new just this last year."

Stewards hoisted the women's luggage aboard. Then each woman was scanned head to toe, credentials and passes checked, and luggage thoroughly checked, before boarding was allowed. At the main deck, they were politely greeted and assigned staterooms. Two women per room. Fortunately, Marlene spoke up, quite persuasively, when Azra was assigned a stateroom with another person other than 'D'. The attendant seemed somewhat irked but consented. Marlene was assigned to be with a woman she had known from London. Everyone seemed pleased.

The opulence and richness of marine design and decor were so impressive one could easily hear gasping as the women descended toward their staterooms. 'D' whispered to Azra, "What a waste to obliterate all this!" Azra quietly responded, "Wonder how much innocent blood was shed to create it!" 'D' just nodded.

9

Stealth & Endurance

The two-day passage from Istanbul to Antalya, through the Dardanelles Strait, would be pleasant enough. The weather was nearly perfect. Early the next morning Shadow loosed its mooring lines and headed into the Sea of Marmara. In less than eight hours they were in the Dardanelles Strait. As they were about to enter the Aegean Sea, Azra saw Ivankov. She spotted him standing on the main deck talking with two other Russians, both in uniforms. Ivankov wore jeans, sneakers, and a black leather car coat.

The men appeared to be arguing over something. Then, by chance, Ivankov turned and when he saw Azra, standing at the rail, did a double take. Azra glanced back and greeted his look with a smile, then turned her gaze toward the far shore, barely visible through a bright sun glancing its brilliance off the water. Like billions of diamonds, glistening on the surface of a turquoise sea.

The three Russians, Ivankov and two military officers returned to their animated chatter. Azra moved away and stepped lively down a ladder to the galley and dining area. As she did, she spotted 'D' talking with a man dressed as a waiter, and a woman in galley garb. She did not stop or interrupt for she knew 'D' was with Mossad agents.

There were several snack bars and two lavish cocktail lounges. Azra made her way to one close by, collected a plate of delicious snacks, and then ordered her favorite concoction, a "Sea Breeze" for a refreshing drink. It was Tonic Water mixed with grapefruit juice.

Seeing two other women sitting at a small table, Azra decided to join them and become acquainted. They had not been visiting more than ten minutes when Ivankov, along with another Russian, also wearing a leather jacket, came into the cocktail lounge and took seats at a table across the room. They were immediately waited on. Azra recognized the waiter as a Mossad agent. All Mossad team images had been studied and committed to memory while at The Bush Compound, and after.

Soon, Ivankov came to where Azra was sitting. With a pleasant look, he spoke in Russian, saying, "You are way too beautiful to be African! You must be British, or Belgian!" Azra responded in Mozambique, "Actually, you idiot, I am African!" Then she offered a lavish smile.

Ivankov looked confused. He did not understand Azra's native tongue. Then, Ivankov asked, "Your language sounds familiar! Do you speak English?" He had asked in the English language. Azra put an even brighter smile on her face, saying, "Why yes! I do quite well, I believe."

Ivankov looked relieved and invited himself to sit. Looking at the other two women, Ivankov asked if they speak English as well. Both affirmed they did, then, turning away from Ivankov, began chatting in German to each other. With a hard stare, Ivankov muttered a Russian slur then looked back at Azra, smiled, and said, "My name is Ivankov. What do they call you?"

"Lily!" And before you ask, if I may, I am from the UK." Azra then smiled while shifting her body, just a little, and crossing her long legs, just to emphasize her feminine qualities. Ivankov noticed. His face relaxed as he began talking of places, happenings, events, and people, which, Azra, quickly discerned were designed to dig into her past. To test her, as to who she was. Then, Ivankov asked, "What language was that you used when I greeted you?"

Azra responded, "It is of ancient origin. Of tribes of eastern Africa which I studied. I use it when I meet total strangers, such as yourself, and am uncertain of their character or motives!" She smiled.

Ivankov scowled and smirked. Then said, "Cute, very cute!" Then added, "I was on business in Mozambique some years ago and it seems your words, in that 'ancient' language are similar."

Azra leaned toward Ivankov, placed her hand on his arm, and said, "Oh you need not be concerned, the language is quite ancient. I can tell you are a Russian gentleman who appreciates the art of cultures!" Then added, "We're here to help you enjoy the time we have together on this beautiful yacht. I trust that will be the case!" Her dark eyes stayed steady, looking into Ivankov's eyes with such controlled tenderness his face again softened. Then he smiled broadly, saying, "You, lovely black lady, are one incredible woman! I look forward to seeing you again. But now I have matters to attend."

Ivankov lifted Azra's hand, kissed it, then turned and left. His friend, who had been sitting, intently observing the conversation, got up and walked out behind Ivankov. As he did, he paused at the opening, and with a hard face, looked back at Azra. Azra instantly recognized him as Dima, Ivankov's bodyguard.

In a manner as not to raise questions from the other two women, Azra slipped her hands below the tabletop and wiped off the hand kiss with her linen napkin. While her outer appearance seemed calm, her inside quivered in icy hatred. One of the women leaned forward and whispered, "Careful of that one!" Azra nodded, understanding, but said nothing about it.

The women rejoined their conversation, and enjoyed fresh drinks, brought to them by the Mossad agent posing as a waiter. He gave a quick look at Azra, then said, in Russian, "Hope you are enjoying yourself.", then smiled and left.

That evening, after a superb dinner, where many vile men and most tainted women who seemed focused on pairing, 'D' and Azra left for their stateroom, went in the bathroom, and talked. Covering voices with shower water and music, just in case the rooms were bugged, 'D' said, "Our gear is aboard. Mossad says they will get our weapons, clothing, and gear from the galley food lockers at 0200. We are to call the galley claiming motion sickness, at 5:30 am the morning we arrive at Antalya, and request some light food, dry crackers, and ginger ale, be brought to the room."

"How safe will that be?" Azra asked.

"It should work just fine. Our guys know what they are doing!" 'D' responded. Then added, "Our agent will take the call and bring it to our room stuffed under a service cart. The door knock will be three sharp taps, followed by two long taps."

"Do we know what time we arrive at Atalya?" Azra asked.

"One of our agents who works on the upper level, says our present ETA will be early morning, estimated to be 0640 hours, the day after tomorrow, June 5th. We're right on schedule!" 'D' Responded. Then she added, "It is he, who will be with me, along with one other, the female agent who boarded at Odessa, when we disarm the anti-aircraft rocket launchers."

"Let's look for the best place to conceal our weapons and gear!" Azra suggested.

"In plain sight!" 'D' smiled as she responded. Then said, "Come, I'll show you." They left the bathroom and went into the stateroom, which was fairly large, with two queen size beds, nightstands, lamps, etc., a lounging area, with a small couch and easy chairs, and a desk and study area, a small bar/kitchenette, plus closets. As she looked around. Azra asked, "Where?" 'D' pointed to where their luggage sat, secured by straps to the bulkhead. Azra smiled and shook her head in agreement.

The next day brought unusually damp weather. A stiff breeze and morning drizzle greeted the women when they attempted to go out to lounge on the main deck. They decided to see more of the yacht, keeping in mind they could only observe certain areas.

On the first upper deck, they passed several smaller rooms, then went into a very large room. At one end, the walls were heavily decorated in medieval armor. An array of shields, swords, and spears were displayed on either side of two oversized suits of polished armor, standing as ancient warriors with spears at the ready. Between them was an opening to a smaller room loaded with ancient artifacts of warfare. The room was designed to be a small theater as well with leather couches, chairs, and tables holding beautiful brass lamps and statuary. Near the entry sat a large, polished mahogany chest with narrow flat-file drawers.

Azra whispered, "Incredible! Like being in a living museum!" Then she went to one of the sword displays, recognizing a beautiful French foil, a 42-inch Spanish Rapier, and a British Sabre. She hefted the Rapier and deftly sliced it through the air, just as a Russian steward appeared.

The Russian introduced himself and politely asked for the Rapier. Azra, just as politely, turned the handle toward the man and handed it to him. Then, as he returned the sword to its place on the wall, held there by magnets, the steward told them of the yacht owner's interest in military history, explaining the origin of several weapons displayed.

"But you are missing some important history, sir!" Azra interrupted.

The steward gave Azra a strange look, then asked, "How so?"

Azra recited several aspects of how each sword was made, the genesis of each in cultures, and the wars where used. The steward was stunned at the knowledge Azra possessed. He was about to say something when 'D' commented, "Then there came the Cossacks! And, with them, the Shaska!" The steward's eyes brightened. He looked at 'D' and then back at Azra. Staring with an obvious sense of pride, he motioned them to follow him to the smaller room where sat the large, polished mahogany chest. Hesitating, the steward pulled out a drawer displaying a brilliant Shaska sword. Next to the sword lay an exquisite leather and brass case.

Azra stepped closer. In a "May I" gesture she sought permission to handle the weapon. The steward nodded approval. Carefully, Azra lifted the Cossack sword and held its gleaming blade high in the air. As she did, a deep Russian voice penetrated the silence, saying, in Russian, "Ah, the lady wishes to become a Cossack!"

Azra and 'D' turned to see a stout man dressed in a white uniform. A uniform resembling a naval officer of rank. The steward quickly took the Shaska from Azra and returned it to the chest, then stood at attention. Azra smiled and responded, in Russian, "Sir, I do believe no Cossack would allow a woman in their ranks. Besides, I would not be of the correct tone of skin, now would I?"

The man laughed, saying, "Right you are on both counts!" Then he added, "My name is Roman. I own this boat. And who might you be? And your lovely friend here?" Roman pointed at 'D' with a short gold and polished wood swagger he was holding.

Azra responded, "My name is Lily Tennison from England and this is my friend, Marlo Casey, she is from Ireland."

"Ah, yes! The escort ladies who have invaded my yacht to make mischief with the men!" Roman jokingly said, then laughed. In a more serious tone, Roman asked, "What is your interest in ancient weapons?"

Azra responded, "I have always had such an interest and studied all I could about swords and ancient weapons."

"Where did you study?" Roman briskly asked.

Azra smiled saying, "Oh, it's a private university called Encyclopedia Brittanica!"

Roman's face brightened. He laughed saying, "Quite famous at that!" Then he asked, "Are you trained in the art of fencing?"

Azra answered, "A little." Then glanced at 'D' who remained stone-faced.

Roman whispered something to a man, Azra assumed him to be a bodyguard, who immediately left the room. Roman continued the strange conversation for a few moments until the man returned. Following him was Anya, the assassin. Following her came Ivankov and his bodyguard Dima. A moment later Marlene, along with three women, escorts, casually walked in.

Roman greeted them, then said, "Well, now that we have a nice little audience, let's have a demonstration!" Turning and pointing to Anya, Roman said, "Lily, meet Anya." Anya flatly responded, "We know each other!" Then Roman, looking at Anya, said, Lily says she is trained somewhat in fencing! Would you care to test her skills?"

Anya smiled a wry smile saying, "Most certainly!" And took off her outer jacket.

Roman then turned to Azra and asked, "Care to demonstrate your talents?"

Azra looked at Roman a second or two then sheepishly said, "I'll certainly try."

Roman laughed loudly, saying, "Great!" Then he shouted, "Everyone to the entertainment room for a little fun!"

They all moved into the large room where weapons were displayed on the walls. Anya immediately went to the swords and picked a foil. Azra walked slowly to the display, looked a moment, and then took the 42-inch Rapier from its wall mount. She then removed a sweater and was left standing in an electric blue blouse with large white poppies. Her pants were desert tan, slightly belled, and wrapped with a gold belt held by an oversized buckle. Her shoes were dress sandals made by Bergdorf Goodman.

Azra stood tall and erect. Looked up and down the Rapier blade, then lowered it to an angle, pointing at the floor. She then, standing absolutely still, looked at Anya, studying her with the eyes of a lioness. Anya was in a classic fencing stance. There she waited a few seconds, then gruffly said, "Well, let's see what you know!"

Azra stood stone-still, her face without expression. She continued her study, focusing on Anya's eyes. She then studied Anya's arms and body, assessing strengths, weaknesses, and most essential, how Anya would telegraph moves. Then, satisfied she had what was needed, Azra moved, slowly, with stealth, like a cat, to her right a few steps, then left, watching Anaya's eyes. Another step to the right, then three to her left, each time inching closer to Anya who was twisting her foil back and forth in an attempt to appear menacing.

Suddenly, the sizzling sound of steel blades embracing filled the room. As Azra anticipated, Anya's eyes telegraphed a move, thrusting her foil at Azra's chest. With one single move of her wrist, Azra sent the foil spinning out of Anya's grasp. It went flying and then hit the floor, sliding to a stop at Roman's feet. Azra pinned the Russian assassin with the point of her blade touching the base of Anya's throat. After a tense few seconds, Azra relaxed the Rapier to a neutral position and slightly bowed.

Except for a curse from Anya, there was silence. The small audience stood gaping in awe. Then, slowly, Roman began to applaud. All others followed his lead. All except Anya who cursed again while grabbing her jacket and left the room.

"Well, Lily, perhaps you *should* seek an appointment with the Cossacks!" Roman shouted. Then said, "I'm having a special dinner this evening, before making port at Antalya. I would be pleased for you and your friend to join us!" Azra looked at 'D' and they both nodded they would attend. Roman shouted, "Good! Excellent show!" and then abruptly left with his bodyguard.

No sooner had Roman left when Ivankov stepped close to Azra and said, "Wow! What other hidden talents do you have?" Azra smiled and gathered her sweater, bowed to the others who, again applauded, and with 'D' went to another part of the yacht to be alone and talk.

A suitable place was found at the stern of the vessel. Drizzle and wind had given way to Mediterranean sparkle.

Azra and 'D' stood silently for a few moments, watching the wake and churn of water as powerful engines plied the yacht through the sea.

Soon, 'D' began to chuckle, saying, "You at least could have allowed her a little warm-up!" They both burst out laughing.

Azra soberly responded, "I just wanted the thing over!"

"Thought you were about to finish her!" 'D' said.

"Thought about it!" Azra said. Then repeated, "Seriously thought about it!"

"What about this dinner with Roman?" Azra asked.

"It's a gift!" 'D' responded. Adding, "We will be in critical areas that provide a view of things we can use when the party begins. Keep your memory sharp as we catalog what we see, and where things are." Azra shook her head in understanding.

Just then Marlene showed up saying, "I've been looking all over for you two!" Then she exclaimed, "Holy Moley Azra, what a show! I'd forgotten your fencing championships! I thought you were going to waste that woman right then and there!"

"Perhaps I should have." Azra flatly responded.

Then Marlene said, "Actually, I have been worried about something and need to say it." She looked down at the deck, then out toward the churning trail Shadow was making through the sea. Her hands were tight on the rail.

"What is it?" 'D' asked.

"Well, it is about the escorts. I wish there was a way to prevent them from harm, at least a chance to get away from what will happen, you know..." Marlene stopped, looked around, and then whispered, "Blowing up this boat!" Then whispering, added, "Several are friends, and I just think they are innocent in this whole affair and should be saved!"

Azra looked at 'D' who stared out to sea with no response, nor expression. Then Azra turned to Marlene saying, "Let us talk this over and see what can be done. There are lots of people involved and chains of command which we must respect."

Marlene looked at 'D' for a second, who did not look back, then turned to Azra and quietly said, "I know you Azra, and trust you'll do what's best." Then walked away.

Azra and 'D' stood at the rail in silence for a few moments. Finally, 'D' said, "There may be a way. I'll mention this to one of our Mossad agents and see if they have any ideas." Then, in a tone of deep concern, shook her head and said, "Damn, this could get very messy for us!"

"There is one thing I recall which may be something to work with." Azra offered.

"What's that?" 'D' Asked.

"There will be a Seal sniper team on a building off the starboard side of Shadow when we are at anchor. I checked and that building is a Monastery. Could it be possible the monks, nuns, priests, whatever, could help in some way?"

"You mean to pray?" 'D' chuckled.

"No, no, I mean to help get those escorts to safety?"

"I know! Just kidding!" 'D' responded. Then she added, "You know, that just may be the only source of land-based help that we could rely on. But how? What manner? What timing? And, how do we let the escorts know without tipping off Bratva and the KGB?"

The two women left to find a snack. Azra suggested the cocktail lounge where she had been before and first met Ivankov. The place was crowded. Seems men and women were getting more acquainted. And, a small band of instrumentalists was playing mellow music, singing some Slovak folk songs in their language. A few were dancing.

As they were collecting meats, and spread for crackers, the Mossad agent posing as a waiter came to the buffet with a fresh platter of fruits and mixed nuts. 'D' was close enough to him, and no one else was around at that moment, so she whispered, "Operation issue we need to discuss!"

The waiter whispered back, "15 minutes at the rail, port side."

When the time arrived, 'D' got up and went to meet with the Mossad agent. Right after she left, Ivankov came into the lounge with Dima, spotted Azra, and made his way through the crowd to where she sat. In Russian, he said, "Well! Here sits Black Beard's sister!" Then, laughing at his own joke, took a seat. Dima took a seat as well, across the small table where Azra sat.

Azra smiled, saying, "You are way, way too kind sir!" Then she looked at Dima and said, "And who might this be your shadow? Your side-kick? No! He must be Tinker Bell! And, you sir" Looking back at Ivankov, "Must be Peter Pan!"

Dima was not laughing. However, Ivankov did laugh, saying, "You're quick!" Adding, "Almost as quick as your Rapier!" Then leaned toward Azra and asked, "How does a woman of your profession learn such skills?" The look in Ivankov's eyes left no doubt he was seriously digging.

"Well, sir, while you were buzzing about with Tinker Bell, I was hobnobbing with Captain Hook!" Azra laughed, a lighthearted, kindly laugh. Then said, "Actually, some years ago, when much younger, I trained for the Olympics and did quite well. Azra then munched on a cracker spread with herbal creamed cheese, topped with a slice of salami.

About then 'D' came back, looked at Azra, and exclaimed, "No fair! You having all the fun!" and sat down close to Dima. Dima looked a little surprised but then spread a toothy smile across his ruddy face, saying, "I'll give you some fun lady!" 'D' pulled back, smiled, and said, "Really! How much fun?" Dima looked at 'D' for a second, laughed, and said, "More than you can handle!"

Then Ivankov asked 'D', "They say you are Irish. Strange, you don't have red hair and you seem to be absent freckles. In fact, you look a little dark! Like, perhaps, from Southern Italy, or maybe further south?"

'D' looked at Ivankov saying, "Here is a little history for you. A long time ago, a Spanish Armada set sail to engage and destroy the British Fleet. A storm frustrated their endeavor and nearly all the vessels sank. Now, a few strong Spaniards swam like crazy for the Irish shore and what do you know, we now have black Irish running about chatting with Pagan

Russians!" 'D' painted a smile on her face and held it until Ivankov finally laughed. It was a short, uncertain laugh.

They chatted a while longer. The conversation was, at times, laced with testy undercurrents. Then a Russian mafia guy, carrying an AK rifle came and whispered something in Ivankov's ear. Ivankov quickly said, "You will excuse us ladies, business!" He motioned to Dima and the two left.

'D' immediately said, "Let's get out of here!" They went directly to their stateroom.

Once certain the room was secure, 'D' said, "Mossad has by now contacted the Seals to assess what may be done to save the escorts. They should be back to us in an hour or so." Then she said, "Something is going on with Bratva and the KGB. They are acting cautious or nervous about something. They may have tracked Conquest in the hacking process and are on alert. We just do not know. But for now, we are on schedule. However, my Mossad contact said, to be ready for anything. He suggested they may try and get our weapons and gear to us tonight and would let us know!"

"I am amazed, frankly, that we have retained security this long. Those Russians are no dummies." Azra responded.

Just then there was a loud knock at the door. 'D' asked who it was. The answer came from Marlene, saying, "It's your party girl!"

'D' opened the door and Marlene, looking a bit frazzled, hurried in. 'D' looked up and down the corridor and saw nothing except a cleaning maid far down to the right.

"Look you guys, I don't know what's going on but the Russians are getting testy!" Marlene whispered.

"Like what, what are they doing?" Azra asked.

"They are searching several of the escorts! Asking questions, checking records, and things like that. I mean real nosey stuff!"

"Okay, Marlene, calm down. We have a pretty strong firewall protecting us and are looking into how best to help your escort friends survive this mission." 'D' took Marlene by the arm and guided her to sit in one of the lounge chairs. Then asked, "Just how would you propose telling the ladies they need to get off the boat and keep it secret?" 'D' asked.

Marlene relaxed, smiled, and said, "You should know! We women have the best grapevine ever invented! We communicate secrets faster than a nuclear chain reaction and were doing it while Oppenheimer was still in diapers! And, no one knew. Especially men!"

Azra sat next to Marlene, took her hand, and quietly said, "Look, dear friend, there may be a way. We should know soon. However, it will fall to the women to do exactly what they are told and when they are told to do it!" Then asked, "Do you understand?"

Marlene soberly responded, "I do!" Then 'D' said, "If whatever is going to be done works, you must also understand that all the women may not make it." 'D' paused, then added, "You may lose some of your friends."

Marlene looked up at 'D', gazed at her for a few seconds, then said, "I trust we all are at risk of not making it. But I know you, and your people, will do the best you can. Just know I'll do my part. Whatever that may be."

There was a knock at the door. 'D' asked who it was and the female voice responding confirmed it was the Mossad agent who was to fly Shadow's helicopter off the pad when the attack order was given. 'D' opened the door and the agent came in, looked at Marlene with suspicion, then, after being assured it was okay to talk, said, "Here are your instructions. Inform escorts they must depart by the boarding ramp which will be lowered for KGB leaders arriving from Moscow tomorrow afternoon at about 1600 hours. They will go down the ramp in groups of six, at 10-minute intervals, beginning at 2230 hours." 'D' interrupted, asking, "Has the start time changed? That's ten minutes sooner!" "I know!" the agent responded. "Our agents and Seal snipers will have cleared the ramp area of guards ten minutes before the command for the main assault."

Then the agent continued, saying, "It's essential only identification papers be carried. No clothing, nothing else!" Then she added, "US Navy Seals will be transporting the women by pontoon craft, taken from Shadow's guards. They will be transported from the yacht to shore, near the monastery. There, they will be received and sheltered by the monks and nuns." Then, looking at 'D', she said, "There will likely be a firefight in progress. Hope all make it but no guarantees!" The agent turned to leave, then stopped and said, "Your gear will be here at midnight!" Then she saluted and left.

"Do you have all that?" Azra asked Marlene. Marlene nodded and shook her head saying, "It's going to be one hell of a night tomorrow!" 'D' then said, "Look Marlene, have you ever seen the movie Sound of Music, where the Von Trapp family exits off stage one at a time to escape the Nazis and run for the Swiss border?"

"Who hasn't seen Sound of Music?" Marlene responded.

'D' then said, "Well, that's what the escorts will be doing! A few at a time will leave the party and, in pretense, powder their noses. But instead, make their way to the ramp and get off this tub! You will need to get this across to them and select who goes and when they go, beginning at 10:30 tomorrow night during the party. They must leave everything behind, except identification documents!"

"Got it!" Marlene said. Then asked, "What about you two?" 'D' glanced at Azra, then said, "We'll be along but in a different direction. There is some business we must attend." With hugs and good wishes, Marlene was about to leave, but turned and whispered, "Sure wish I could be at that dinner tonight!" then she left.

The two women warriors put on a different kind of war paint for the evening. 'D' loosed her hair, letting her full dark mahogany locks fall past her shoulders. Both dressed in their most alluring apparel. Azra was in a deep red silk dress that formed every subtle curve of her tall body. 'D' dressed in a rich purple set of tights with a flowing cape that made her appear as a fully formed fairy. Her wavy hair presented just the right touch of class. Both selected gold bracelets and modest gold necklaces with a cluster of small emeralds for Azra and diamonds for 'D'.

At the appointed hour, they made their way to the upper deck, and dining room, where they would sit and dine with some of the most vile people on the planet and dine. On their way, guards and staff expressed sufficient lust to confirm the women were absolutely beautiful. And when they entered the private and beautifully decorated dining room, all the men stood, except one. Azra glanced at him, instantly recognizing the man to be Lev Morozoy, head of Bratva. *How could such a short and common-looking man control so much evil in the world?* Azra thought to herself. Then another thought crossed her mind; *"Napoleon!"*

Roman invited Azra to sit next to him. Ivankov, with a smile revealing his being much impressed, sat directly opposite Azra. Dima sat next to 'D', by invitation of Roman. Lev sat with a scowl, glaring back and forth at the two women. There were several other women present, some were escorts. One Azra had met when first in the cocktail lounge the day before. She smiled.

Looking about, there sat three Russian Army officers and two men who smelled of being KGB. But the most revealing evil attending were four other men, a drug lord from Serbia, an international syndicate gun dealer from Ukraine, a human trafficker from Syria, and a mercenary chief from Slovenia. Each had a woman who was not of the group of escorts. At the far end sat other men, they were Alexander, Alexi, Sergi, Victor, and then Anya. Bratva's top goons and other men were sitting with escorts. Each was recognized from Intel provided by the CIA. And here they all were. A gaggle of murderous vultures, sitting together on a $750 million Russian Yacht and embedded with the Russian government.

Gesturing toward 'D', Azra, and the other women, Roman graciously commented how such beauty enhanced his yacht. How much talent, as witnessed earlier when Azra crossed swords with Anya, had elevated energy! Then with a nod, a string of waiters entered displaying a lavish assortment of Hors d'oeuvres and selections of wines, beers champagne, and, the best of Russia's Vodka, "*Jewel of Russia, Ultra Black*". Among the waiters were two Mossad agents.

When all had their crystal glasses filled with their preferred drink, a toast was offered. Roman stood saying, "Comrades, and ladies, tomorrow, at Antalya, we shall host the very elite of Russia, men who successfully advance our cause and soon will champion that cause in Africa, Indonesia, and the Islands for Father Russia!" All stood, raised their glasses, and sent a hearty Russian cheer echoing in and out of the room.

The dinner was an assortment of upland game; pheasant, grouses, quail, and duck, prepared in exquisite dishes only five-star chefs know how to present. There was no doubting the oligarchy status Roman held among such scum.

After over two hours of talking, with stuffed mouths, over who would do what in schemes to take over Indonesia and East Africa; and, after several fills of libation, Roman began to suggest his night would be aptly enjoyed with Azra's company.

Ivankov noticed the advances. He also could tell Roman was well on his way to total intoxication and soon found an opportunity to pull Azra aside for a private chat. Azra thanked him. Then asked, "I'm hearing several of our sister escorts are being examined. What's that all about?" Ivankov had consumed his share of drink as well and was loose with his response, saying, "Nothing really! We had word from those KGB clowns over there that our security systems may have been penetrated. It's all fluff! We're totally impenetrable on this ship…yacht!" Then burped and laughed. Followed by shouting, "Superfood!" toward Roman then laughed again.

Azra looked over at 'D' who gestured it was time to leave. Dima was nearly ready to pass out! Looking around, Azra saw Lev depart with one of the escorts. Roman was snoring. The KGB guys were arguing and the Russian officers had long gone from the table. The drug lord, gun runner, trafficker, and mercenary were engrossed in their conversations, laughing and treating their girlfriends like dirt. In all, the dinner had become as decadent as pagan follies!

Turning to Ivankov, Azra politely said, "I need to use a restroom. Please excuse me." Ivankov's eyes were half closed. He waved Azra off saying, "No problem lady!" Then, his words slurring, said, "Need help just let me know!" He chuckled, then coughed while uttering a vile slur.

Azra left. 'D' was right behind her. They checked the time and saw it was near midnight. "The gear!" "D' whispered. Near running, they headed to their stateroom. On the way, a guard saw and challenged them. "If you really want to know who we are and what we are doing, I'll ask Roman to chat with you! Okay?" Azra flatly said. The guard motioned them on.

Within moments after arriving, there was a tapping at the door. Three sharp taps, two long. Azra opened the door and was greeted by a smiling Mossad agent holding a cart in front of him. In English, he said, "Late-night snack ladies?"

Azra invited him in. In seconds, the agent had two duffels pulled from under the cart. Turning to 'D' he spoke in a whisper, using Hebrew. He said nothing to Azra. Just saluted and calmly said, "Enjoy the party!"

'D' opened one of the duffels, looked, and handed it to Azra, saying, "This one is yours!" Opening the other duffel, 'D' pulled out a headset for communications and put it on. After a few adjustments, she called, saying, "K2 here!" She motioned for Azra to do the same, to get her headset on and log in. As soon as Azra had her earpiece working, she said, "L3 here!"

"Gaza 1 to team. Conditions critical! Maintain earpieces for communication at all times! Stay alert! Instructions at 0600 tomorrow! Gaza 1 out!"

The message was short but revealed a problem had or was developing. "Typically a security issue!" 'D' whispered.

Azra looked at 'D' for a moment saying, "Not much we can do about it tonight. Let's get some sleep. We're going to need the rest tomorrow…or today. It's after midnight!".

'D' shook her head in agreement. But instead of heading for bed, she pulled out her weapons and gear, laid them on the bed, and closely examined every piece, including her bulletproof vest, her Beretta 9mm, an IWI Jerico 941 automatic pistol chambered for .45 caliber, as backup, a Stoner SR-25 automatic sniper rifle, five grenades, and two fighting knives. Plus night vision gear and a handset for optional communications capabilities.

Curiosity took hold of Azra. She pulled her duffle to her bed and after laying everything out, said, "We are going to war!" Azra also had a Beretta 9mm, and other weapons and gear, about the same as 'D'. However, instead of a Stoner SR-25, she was given a Colt CAR-15 Commando Sub-Machine Gun. And a Heckler & Koch, .45 automatic pistol as backup. The Car-15 was fitted with a silencer.

The two women went to bed. Whispered "what ifs" for another half an hour, then let sleep take them into a somewhat redeeming rest away from the stench of evil they had endured that evening at Roman's diner.

10

Tulip, Tulip, Tulip

Shadow arrived at Antalya Harbor early; two hours earlier than scheduled. The silence, lack of engines humming, and sea sounds brought Azra straight up in bed. In less than two seconds, 'D' followed. A quick look out of the porthole confirmed they were at anchor at Antalya. The security pontoon boats were already deployed. Guards paced about the yacht with weapons at the ready.

On shore, hundreds of people stood gawking, pointing, and yammering about the huge, beautiful yacht that now occupied their small harbor. As hoped, the Monastery was seen from the porthole meaning the bow of the ship was pointed toward the sea. Beyond the Monastery were red tile rooftops for about as far as one could see. The town was definitely bigger than expected. Cursed by the dinge of smog hanging lifeless in stagnant air.

"Go ahead and shower, Azra." I'm going to snooze a few moments!" 'D' said as she climbed back in bed. Azra glanced out of the porthole once more, then said, "Shower can wait, I'm going to sack it for a while." The two women drifted back to an uneasy sleep, but not for long. No more than fifty minutes passed when a sharp knocking at the door brought them instantly awake, upright in their beds.

'D' and Azra grabbed their Berettas which they kept close under their pillows. The rapid knock came again. Azra went to the door saying, "Who is it?" A muffled response confirmed it was Marlene.

When Azra opened the door, Marlene pushed Azra aside. Azra looked and spotted a guard with another man far down the corridor. They were walking slowly, the guard carrying an AK. The other seemed not to have a weapon, at least that showed. Azra squinted in the dim light and then realized the other man was Dima, Ivankov's bodyguard. Quickly, and quietly, Azra closed and locked the door, then whispered for Marlene to shush as she was jabbering about something to do with the escorts.

'D' was up and had slipped on a robe. She grabbed Marlene who looked frazzled and sat her in a chair then pressed fingers to her lips indicating silence. Azra whispered who was coming their direction to 'D'. 'D' quickly fluffed her hair and whispered for Marlene to get in the shower stall and squat on the floor. Then motioned for Azra to get into bed and pretend to be asleep. In a flash, both Azra and Marlene were where they needed to be. A few seconds later there was a soft knock on the door. 'D' remained silent. The knock came again. Louder, more solid!

In a voice mimicking a waking person, 'D' called out, "Who is it?" Dima answered, announcing himself, then saying, "Hey Marlo! Just wanted to check and see if you are okay! And, have a message for Lily from Ivankov."

"We are doing fine. Thank you. It's early and we are asleep!" 'D' responded.

"Open the door, please, we need to be certain. Besides, I need to deliver the message personally to your friend Lily!"

"Okay! Just a moment!" 'D', sounding a little irked, responded.

'D' looked at Azra, checked with Marlene, and then went to the door. She unlocked it, opened it a little, and said, "Dima, it's so early! What's happening?"

Dima poked his head in a little, looked over at Azra who was sitting up but had her Beretta firmly in hand under the covers, then looking back at 'D' said, 'Sorry about last night, guess I had a few too many!" Then smiled. As he did, he handed an envelope to 'D' and said, "This is for your friend from my boss!"

Smiling, Dima then said, "See you at the party tonight?"

'D' smiled back politely saying, "Wouldn't miss it!" Then she asked, "What's all the security checks about? What's going on? Are we in danger?"

Dima cleared his throat a little, then said, "Well, it's the KGB. Those idiots are totally paranoid. They think we have a spy aboard and have us chasing our tails."

"What!" 'D' exclaimed. "Why would a spy be on this yacht? Starving for a party or something?"

"I know! I know!" Dima responded. "But we have to go through the motions, you know, check here and there, look under lifeboat covers, on and on! Even toilets and showers!" Then he posed a fake serious look, smiled, and asked, "Anyone in your shower Marlo?"

'D' responded, 'I can assure you, Dima, last time I showered, it was only me, myself and I in that shower!"

Dima smiled all the more saying, "Too bad! I think I'd enjoy being with you.

'D' just smiled. Then said, "See you this evening!"

Dima muttered he was looking forward to it as well. Then, waving at Azra, said, "Excuse the early call, pretty lady!" Dima left and 'D' closed and locked the door, then, after handing the envelope to Azra, sat down and exhaled. All the time, in one hand, she had her Beretta held behind her. She sat it down, gently, on the coffee table.

Azra got Marlene out of the shower and the three of them sat a moment together, saying nothing. 'D' finally spoke, saying, "Well, what does Ivankov have to say? Azra opened the envelope, read it, then handed it to 'D'. After a moment, 'D' looked at Azra, saying, "They have intelligence alright, but not enough to precisely act on." Sounds like they are swatting at flies." Azra responded, 'Right! But if they use shotguns, they are going to hit something and we need to be certain it's not us!"

Marlene then spoke, saying, "That's what I needed to tell you. I have informed all the escorts. They, all except two, are willing, I'd say, anxious, to get off the boat. Those other two do not, or choose not, to believe or accept what I have told them. But I think it will work! It's just that the girls are super nervous."

'D' checked her watch, motioned to Azra, and said, "Marlene, you need to excuse us. Please go back to your stateroom and we will get together at breakfast, say at 8:30 in the main dining hall?" Marlene nodded. At the door, she turned to Azra and smiled saying, "You really should try the shower thing!" 'D' scooted her out. Then turned to Azra, smiled, and said, "Your friend worries me…a lot!"

After Marlene left, 'D' asked, "What do you think about Ivankov's request that you and he meet in the weapons display room tonight, same place where you taught Anya a lesson, or two?"

Azra responded, "Don't like it!" Then added, but perhaps I can stall it until tonight during the party. Then again, I may have him exactly where I want him!" Azra read the note again, shook her head, and said, "At his request, even! Interesting!"

The morning was quite pleasant. Azra went about, among all the escorts, who were having morning coffee, orange juices, or tonic waters with *Alka-Seltzer*, doing their best to give them assurances they would be alright if, and she emphasized the *if*, they did exactly as told that evening.

Then Azra and 'D' sat together with Marlene, enjoying a sumptuous breakfast. They discussed essential information received by a transmission that morning at 0600 from Gaza 1. The exit timing for the escorts was moved up by thirty minutes. That meant Seal snipers would be covering them. They were to exit Shadow and board pontoon craft the Seals secured from Shadow's guards just before when the first group of women got to the bottom of the ramp. The surveillance shutdown by Conquest would be coordinated with that timing.

'D' then said, "Look, Marlene, shortly after the ladies begin leaving, the assault order will be given. That's when all escorts need to be headed down the ramp and boarding. If there's a problem with the pontoon craft, then swim the 100 yards for the shore where monks and nuns will be waiting to help."

Marlene responded, "I'll do my best. I promise! But what about you guys? What can I do to help you?" Almost in unison, Azra and 'D' responded, "Absolutely nothing!" Then Azra added, "You are a dear friend, Marlene, you just get down that ramp and into the Monastery! We'll connect again when this is over!"

Just then Ivankov walked into the room, looked around, and spotting Azra came directly to where she, 'D', and Marlene were sitting. Looking at Marlene he grinned and said, "That red hair reminds me of someone I once knew in Paris." Then, looking at Azra, said, "I assume you read my note?" Azra nodded that she had.

Ivankov pulled up a chair next to Azra and continued, "There are high-level friends from Moscow, the Kremlin, actually, arriving this afternoon. I'd like you to meet them and they want to meet you before the party begins! In fact, they have suggested you be invited to join the KGB. They know you speak exotic African languages which could be very useful to our business interests on that continent! They are here to discuss that venture in a meeting with Bratva later tonight!"

Ivankov ordered coffee, then continued. "Look, Lily, I must remain with them while the entertainment is happening!" Then he said, "I'll be looking for you in the armor collection room where we can talk. There are a few things I want to discuss in private. My friends will join us soon after. It would be a good place for introductions." What time? Azra asked. Ivankov glanced at his watch, then said, "About 9:30 should work. Just wait for me in case I'm a little late! But I'm never late!"

Azra responded, "It would be an honor to meet your Kremlin friends." Then smiled, saying, "I wait ten minutes for those holding a bachelor's degree, twenty minutes if they have a master's degree, and, well, as long as it takes if they have a Ph.D." Ivankov looked dumbfounded for a second or two, then smiled back, saying, "I have them all!"

"Really?" Azra responded. "Wow, professor Ivankov! And just what is the late meeting about, a new science, rockets, or discovery of oil, or perhaps ancient treasure?" Ivankov started to say something but changed his mind. Instead, he smiled and said, "Oh, should you be included, I'm sure you'll find it interesting!" Then added, "Good, then, until tonight!" He bade a good morning to the three women and left.

While Ivankov was there, 'D' caught a glimpse of a shoulder-holstered handgun under his jacket. She leaned over to Azra saying, "He's left-handed! A gun is on his right side! Remember, left-handed!" Azra sarcastically repeated Ivankov's' words, "I have them all!" 'D' and Marlene laughed. Then, soberly, Azra whispered, "He's as dangerous as any Cobra!"

The day seemed long. Anxious emotions, deadly conditions, and fluid activities have an unseemly way of slowing time. The kind of slow motion appearing devilish, even menacing! It can distort realities and bring about unwanted consequences. Azra and 'D' had every hope the escorts would hold it together and most essential, none would accidentally, or intentionally, spill their guts about the attack just hours away. The balance of security had become razor-thin!

"Let's go over it again!" Azra said. 'D' looked at Azra saying, "The clock for us begins at 9:15 in the Amory display room. That's where we'll stage weapons and gear. We block surveillance cameras. You take down Ivankov when he arrives at about 9:30. You and I deal with the other Russians who are coming sometime after him. Then you head for the party and help Mossad agents take down Bratva leaders and any KGB we have spotted. By that time Conquest will have power down so we'll need our night vision on. I'll be helping disarm the anti-aircraft rocket launcher. Then we get to the helicopter pad and board the Blackhawk as it touches down. You may be ahead of me but I will follow as soon as I know Lev Morozoy is either cuffed and gagged and ready for transport or he is dead!"

Shaking her head, Azra commented. "There are several variants! I suppose all we can do is stay flexible and play it as it comes!"

"Yes, dear friend!" 'D' responded. "But remember this, if this thing begins to go south on us, we have two choices. Either get to the helicopter pad or dive off this boat and swim for shore! The one thing I am counting on is the Navy Seals. Surely they will be watching from sniper positions and cover us if need be!" The two women looked at each other. Their minds tingled with the intensity of high-voltage wires. Then, together, they stood and embraced. Azra smiled and whispered, "I'm hungry!"

Azure skies, stars appearing bright, and balmy air belied chaos and destruction awaiting servants of a godless nation. Escorts were feeling increasingly anxious. Nerves were beginning to spill beyond capacity to disguise themselves as consenting participants in the fun and games. The slender thread holding it all together was a Rock Band from Romania. Nearly everyone was bouncing, laughing, joking, while staying within the trench of decadent pleasures. The band was terrific. The show was magnetic! They had all the best of rock-n-roll down solid. *Suicide Blonde, Doubleback, Hard to Handle, and Wicked Game*, all came off with such energy, slathered with booze, and pot, that Shadow, itself, seemed to Rock!

Back-to-back, while dancing, Azra shouted to 'D', "Time to powder noses!" They left the spacious floor, jammed with jumping bodies, leaving whoever they were dancing with clueless! Down a corridor, then down two more levels, using a mirrored elevator, the two women made their way to the stateroom.

Using a utility cart, they carried their gear up to the ancient amor room and, after smearing security cameras with Vaseline, set the duffels behind one of the couches. 'D' found a place to hide. A storage closet close by was perfect for 'D' to keep an eye on Azra. It was 9:23.

"Hey, Lily, see you made it okay. Sorry, I'm a bit late. My friends are super engrossed with a couple of your lovely friends!" Ivankov was dressed in a black silk suit and black tie. His patent leather shoes flashed in the soft light from the several table lamps.

"You look like you are going to a funeral!" Azra quietly said. Then she laughed, saying, "That is some band you guys found for the party! Some band!"

"Hey, they were hard to get and cost a fortune! Cargo has top ratings and knows its stuff! Right?"

As she moved toward the mahogany chest, Azra responded, "Sure do. Wild!" Then asked, "What is it you want to talk about!"

"Two things, sweet black lady. First I choose you to be with me tonight. And second, it would be terrific if you would join Bratva and tell the KGB, 'Thanks but no thanks!' Then said, "Look babe, with you in Bratva, we could have a blast doing some crazy stuff all over this planet. Some incredible adventures and you would be totally wealthy...totally!" Ivankov was in his Russian macho element, thinking he had complete sway over Azra.

With her back toward Ivankov, Azra pulled out the drawer holding the Shaska Cossack sword, held it up in the air, twisted it back and forth, and then with a giggle, said, "Do you think I could join the Cossacks as well?"

"Sure!" Ivankov responded. "Whatever your lovely heart desires!"

Ivankov had stepped close to Azra and was about to slip an arm around her waist from behind when Azra suddenly twisted about and set the tip of the razor-sharp blade under Ivankov's chin. Her voice came in the low growl of a lioness as she said, "Where you are going, there is no blast!" She pressed the blade, drawing blood, but did not thrust it up through his skull.

Ivankov jerked back and reached for his gun. In a flash, in one vicious stroke, Azra struck the blade across his left arm, severing it from his body. Ivankov screamed and fell back a few paces. As he did, Azra kept a steady pace with him and sliced the Cossack blade down Ivankov's chest. His white shirt gushed red from blood. Azra, in the same growling tone, said, "For my father, Eka!" Ivankov's eyes budged with fear, then flipped to anger, as he shouted, "Who in hell are you?"

"My great, great, grandfather was The Lion of Gaza! "I'm the Lioness of Gaza! And, you, you piece of slime, are finished messing with my family!" With that Azra twirled in a karate move, holding the blade straight out with both hands and severed Ivankov's head. His frame slumped to the floor. The head rolled to the foot of one of the polished armor suits and stopped, face down. Azra let the Shaska drop to the floor, stood still, and then, as the adrenalin rush peaked, shivered. But only slightly.

'D' came to Azra and held her hand. In that same moment, they heard voices and looked out of the room seeing two well-dressed men walking briskly while talking, toward them. The men were so engrossed; that they did not take a clear look at what was lying on the floor. One, in fact, when he saw the clump of clothing, laughed, saying, "Someone lost his suit!" The other began to laugh but stopped when he realized the shine on the floor was reflections off a pool of blood. They both looked at 'D' who had her Beretta fitted with a silencer, pointed directly toward them. They froze. 'D' fired two shots each, dropping the Kremlin officials where they stood.

As fast as possible, Azra and 'D' shed party clothes and got into their military suits with vests. After strapping on headgear with night vision, and lacing weapons to leg slings, the two female warriors ran toward the corridor. As they did, Dima suddenly appeared. With a look of complete shock, he braced himself and grabbed for his weapon. Before he could swing it into a position to fire, he had been hit six times. Three shots were fired from Azra. Three from 'D'! Ten seconds later, the lights went out!

"Conquest is on the job!" 'D' hollered. Then said, "See you at the helicopter pad!" and ran up a ladder toward the upper decks. Azra waved and made her way, carefully, toward the party, the Romanian Rock band, and the remaining Bratva goons. Just as she arrived, her earpiece came alive. "This is Gaza 1, TULIP, TULIP, TULIP!" After that, Gaza 2 came on, saying, "All units take down primary targets!"

Instantly, gun flashes and loud reports of, mostly handguns, revealed the attack was underway. As she entered the room, she spotted Viktor crouching near a table. With two shots he lay prone, jerking, coughing blood! As she bumped and thrashed her way through the crowd, she spotted Lev but then lost sight of him. Seconds later, Azra came face to face with Sergi who had a gun in hand, waving it around in confusion. She was about to fire when she was hit from behind by another man trying to flee the bedlam. The man fell on top of Azra and then scrambled to get up. As he did, he stepped on Azra's arm.

Azra got up, shook her arm, which was bruised but not broken, and then looked again for Sergi. An instant later she spotted him exiting toward the galley. Azra ran through the thinning crowd and caught up with Sergi just as he was about to exit into a passageway. Two headshots dropped the Russian. Even as the dead man was falling, Azra heard someone scream, "Azra, watch out!" It was Marlene. Azra turned to see the assassin Anya was about to stab her in the back with a large butcher knife. Her right hand was still in the air, holding the knife. But protruding from her stomach was a long skewer for roasting chickens.

Anya gasped and fell to the floor, Marlene stood frozen in shock. At that moment, a severely injured Anya reached under her skirt, and pulled out a small automatic pistol, firing three shots into Marlene. Azra was not able to see what had happened until too late. But, instantly, Azra emptied what bullets remained of her 15-round magazine into the assassin. Then knelt next to Marlene, pulled her head up, and brushed her red hair away from her face, saying, "Oh dear Marlene! You should have gone with the others." Marlene coughed, spit a little blood, and whispered, "Came looking for you. Did I do well? Tell me, did I do well?" Suddenly Marlene gripped Azra's arm and stiffened in exquisite pain, then slowly gave out her final breath.

Sobbing, Azra looked at Marlene, whose spirit had departed and quietly said, "You did well, very well, dear friend. An explosion somewhere above on the yacht shook the galley causing kettles, pans, and utensils to fall and clatter across the floor.

Through the haze and dim light from the yachts' red night-running lighting, 'D' suddenly appeared. She slid to where Azra knelt, grabbed her by the arm, and shouted, "We need to go, now!" Azra, sobbing, shook her off and pulled Marlene to her chest. Again, 'D' took hold of Azra saying, "We need to get to the pad!"

Reluctantly, Azra let Marlene recline. Then stood and spit on Anya's dead body. Azra turned and ran with 'D' toward a passageway and then to a ladder leading up to the helicopter pad. "What was the explosion?" Azra shouted. "We had trouble getting wiring figured out to disable the missile launcher. I told the agent to head for cover, pulled a phosphorous grenade, and stuffed it down the launch tube! Did the job!"

Just as the two women emerged at the helicopter pad, a Russian KGB agent fired at them with an AK. He missed. Azra ducked behind a large vent cowling and 'D' jumped back into the passageway. While they could see each other, they could not see the agent. 'D' readied to make a move and join Azra. As she did, she became fully exposed to the agent who stood with feet spread apart, his AK at the ready. He smiled and was about to pull the trigger when his body appeared to explode. In that instant, The Mossad Cobra hovered over, the pilot offering a salute.

Azra and 'D' made their way to the pad but the Black Hawk was gone. "Gaza 2, this is K2, come in!" "K2, this is Gaza 2, where are you?" "K2 to Gaza 2, at the HP." "K2, stay put, we'll come and get you! Where is L3?" "K2 to Gaza 2, with me!" "Are you injured?" "Gaza 2, we are fine, hurry, K2 out!" A moment later, "K2 this is Gaza 2, Kacatka on its way, two minutes out. Be ready to board! Gaza 2 out!"

Azra looked off toward the Monastery with her night vision. She saw several women being helped up the bank and into the compound. Then spotted three bodies floating in the water. Two had suitcases floating next to them. One still had a grip on hers.

"Come on L3, the bird is about to land!" Azra looked along the decks of the yacht spotting at least ten dead guards. Among them were two bodies of women. Suddenly the wind-blast of rotor blades off the Russian helicopter caused Azra to focus and in seconds they were pulled aboard and greeted by two Mossad agents. The Kacatka lifted vertically then, tilted, and flew toward the open sea, accelerating to gain as much speed and distance as possible. Seconds later, they heard a command on their headsets. "Gaza 2, extraction complete, target clear, charges set. Detonate. Detonate. Detonate!"

Seconds passed before a fireball erupted, splitting darkness with crimson and orange flames, lighting up the entire harbor and most of the city. A few seconds later, a shockwave hit the helicopter, causing it to wobble. 'D' was staring at the floor shaking her head and muttering. Azra asked what was wrong. 'D' responded, "Lev, I did not get Lev!" Azra responded, "Well, surely, the explosion took care of that problem!" They looked at each other; looked with expressions of doubt, a fainting sort of doubt leaving an acrid emptiness.

A little over an hour later, the lights of Akrotiri and the British RAF base brought thoughts of family and being a step closer to home. As they landed, Azra noticed the Van Steenwijk jet, a Gulf Stream 600, parked near a large hanger. Standing near the plane were Rowland and the kids, Terresa and Tommy. Also standing close by were Tracey and Elsje with their Indonesian flight attendant. All vigorously waving.

Also nearby, sat the Black Hawk and Cobra. The Mossad team, with gear scattered about, were clustered together, rejoicing. All had made it without serious injury. Two were wounded, One a hand wound, the other, a bullet through his thigh. Gaza 2 drew their attention to the Kacatka as it touched down.

A Mossad agent opened the door. With a smile, using words from a Jewish prayer/song, in Hebrew he said, *"The tempest is tossed. Welcome to the lamp at Golden Shores!"* 'D' reached over and kissed the man on his cheek. Azra did the same, saying, "Thank you!" Then the two women exited the Russian helicopter.

A daring and skillful warrior and daughter of Abraham. And, the Lioness of Gaza stood still, observing, sensing the realities of being alive. As they did, cheers erupted! Family, friends, and fellow warriors had fought tenacious evil forces and prevailed.

Some British officers came to the hangar where everyone was gathered. They commended the Mossad agents, Azra, and 'D' for their good work. A doctor and nurse attended to the two men injured, replacing temporary dressings with the best they had.

A few moments later the unmistakable sounds of a C-130 Hercules landing came to ear. Moments later the plane, with markings of the Star of David, rolled up on the tarmac. 'D' looked at Azra and Rowland, saying, "This may not be timely or proper notice, but I've decided to return to Mossad." Azra threw her arms around 'D' saying, "You always will have a home with us!" Rowland hugged 'D' as well, saying, "You're incredible!" Then Terresa and Tommy hugged 'D' tight! 'D' leaned down saying to Tommy, "Hang on to your Yoda! He will watch for the bad guys and warn you!" Then turned to Terresa saying, "Give yourself a little time before growing up. It's okay to enjoy your childhood!"

With help from several IMF men and women, the Mossad team's gear was hauled to the Hercules. Then the Mossad team began moving toward the plane. As they did, each one saluted Azra. 'D', who had joined them, waved one last time as she paused on the ramp. Soon the C-130 raced down the runway and was in the air, headed for Israel.

Shortly after, the Gulfstream 600, just as the first sign of dawn became visible, was airborne. The sleek jet streaked through the sky, climbing to 37,000 feet in less than 18 minutes, then higher, to 45,000 feet. At near Mach one speed, the Gulfstream headed for Maputo where Rowland, Azra, and the kids would be delivered home. Then, to Jakarta, to the Van Steenwijk home, where pressing matters awaited for Elsje to help resolve.

In moments, Azra fell sound asleep in one of the large leather lounge chairs which reclined into a bed. Rowland placed a down comforter over her, leaned over, and gently kissed her forehead, which caused Azra to slightly awaken. She looked up, smiled a little, and whispered, "I so love you!" Rowland kissed her again, saying, "Sleep, precious, sleep!"

11

Solitude

"I cannot believe this!"

"What?" Elsje askes Tracey.

"They are killing all the goats on Catalina Island! That's what!" Tracey responds as he launches his lanky body off the couch and walks toward the kitchen while holding a week-old copy of the Los Angeles Times.

"Why would they?" Elsje asks, wiping her hands dry with a dish towel.

'Greenies'! They say goats eat too much vegetation and are denuding the island!"

"Well. Are they?" Elsje quips.

"Well, they do reproduce nearly as fast as rabbits! They do eat just about anything, and likely could strip the island clean! But, *dearest*, they also keep the rattlesnake population under control on that island! Besides, they have been there since around 1840, perhaps earlier!" Rowland was struggling to present a case.

Elsje put her arm around Tracey's neck, looked him square in the eye, and asked, "Are you now the intrepid defender of Catalina Goats?" Tracey smiled but said nothing.

The fragrance of tropical flowers beckoned Tracey to the upper veranda at the Van Steenwijk home. The grounds were in top condition and a light breeze off the water mixed nature's relaxing fragrances into a concoction that could soothe the hackles of any man.

Tracey was becoming uneasy. They had remained in Jakarta for nearly two months after the raid on Bratva aboard the yacht Shadow. And, while his Real Estate Company was running as slick as sewing machine oil, he felt a little out of the loop!

"Wonder how the girls are doing at home in Long Beach?" Rowland shouted.

"Call them and find out!" Elsje shouted back.

"It's nearly 3:00 am Pacific Time! Think I'll wait!"

Elsje came to where Tracey was standing, slipped her arms around him, and whispered, "Thinking of heading for Long Beach?"

"The thought has crossed my mind but you have so much to do here…well, going home to Long Beach can wait."

"Actually, dear," Elsje said, "we may be able to leave sooner than planned. The matters we were struggling to resolve for three of the ships, and a new captain and crew, are fairly resolved, except for details, and the V.P.'s can work them out. So, Mr. Schaffer, when you call the girls, tell Sophia and Isabella we shall be coming soon and we will let them know when flight schedules are arranged!"

"Really!" Tracey responded. Then he added, "Well now, I just may form a 'Protect the Goats Society' and march on Avalon City Hall!"

As Elsje returned downstairs, she chuckled and said, "It will likely be the shortest march in history!"

Rowland, Azra, and the kids were home in Maputo. The fishing and canning were doing well. In fact, better than ever before. Rowland, Azra, and Adelia, who remained active in running the company, decided to add two additional, and more modern, fishing vessels to their fleet. More orders from additional countries had created the demand for more fish. And, the three canning plants were reaching capacity.

'D' had contacted Azra saying she had been assigned to East Africa and several countries near the Black Sea. It is a territory she knew well. She would serve as operations chief with Mossad. 'D' also disclosed that Lev was seen in Odessa and photographed. No word on how he escaped the yacht. But several Turkish people at the Monastery had seen a man being picked out of the water by fishermen near the harbor entry at Antalya. Azra said 'D' thought it likely was Lev! It was certain the head of Bratva was still alive!

Ten days had passed when Elsje came back from the office announcing her urgent work with the company was complete. It was time to head for Long Beach. Together, she and Tracey called the girls and let them know when they would arrive, asking them to meet them at the LAX International Terminal, the KLM Airlines arrival area.

Sophia and Isabella were thrilled their parents were returning. Soon, the two girls would need to leave for university studies and work. Sophia had a new assignment in Brussels where she would handle marketing for Van Steenwijk Shipping to several countries in Western Europe.

Sophia was older than Isabella by three years. She is a beautiful blonde girl, is tall and outgoing, loves sports, is an expert archer, enjoys dancing, and sings beautifully with a soprano voice trained in the classical style.

Her bachelor's degree in business and international marketing from the University of San Diego was all she wanted or needed to launch herself into the Van Steenwijk Company. And, quickly became a highly valued asset.

Isabella, five foot, 6 inches tall, with lovely features, and long auburn hair, most often tied in a loose bun, is quiet, reserved, and focused on science and mathematics. She has one of the highest IQ ratings ever recorded during testing when she was just 15 years old.

Isabella became an accomplished pianist at eight years old and is often asked to participate in recitals at the university and elsewhere. She has completed her thesis and is on track to receive a Master's in Nuclear Physics at MIT. However, Isabella is a bit torn between accepting a position offered at NASA or going for a PhD. Be that as it may, both girls were excited to have time with their parents as summer was beginning to drift into fall. Time, as they both pleaded, "Aboard Fair Wind!" Among all things considered, they both loved sailing and had sailed since babies.

Flight time from Jakarta to LAX took about 20 hours with a connecting flight at Singapore. The trip is exhausting for anyone of any age. But the Van Steenwijk jet was needed elsewhere so Tracey and Elsje accepted the realities of commercial flying which, with so much security was becoming increasingly tiresome. Fortunately for them, they were able to reserve first class. Even so, airlines all over the world were finding ways to engineer tighter seating and less service. Flying had become bussing!

"I see them!" Sophia excitedly said.

Isabella responded, "I see them as well. They look a little haggard!" "Yes," Sophia responded. Then added, "Such is our world…haggard flying!" Then chuckled.

Though Tracey and Elsje were still some distance away, Sophia and Isabella both waved. Elsje smiled and nudged Tracey who had his head down. They smiled and waved back! A moment later they were hugging, chatting, and walking toward the luggage carousels. On the way, Elsje asked about the house and garden. Both girls responded, "Everything was just fine." But, Isabella added, "Roy has used a small area to grow some veggies!" Elsje and Tracey responded, "Really!" Isabella continued, "You will not believe the tomatoes and corn…so good!"

Soon they were in the limo. The driver loaded their luggage and away they went. Just as they were about to exit the airport Tracey buzzed the driver on the car phone. The driver answered. His voice was heavily laced with either Eastern European, Slovick, or Russian accent. Tracey looked at Elsje and she looked at him. Pausing a second, Tracey said, "Take Highway One…the Pacific Coast route, down to Long Beach, I want to decompress along that old route and not sit on the freeway!" It was 3:30 pm. Rush hour, actually, rush hour plus four, was in progress. The driver responded, "Yes sir, Mr. Tracey."

Elsje and Tracey, again, looked at each other. Then Tracey looked at the girls and asked, "Is this our usual limo service, the one we normally order?" Both answered that it was. "This fellow, when he picked you up, did he ask questions, that is, was he inquiring of anything personal, you know, what you do and so forth."

Sophia responded, saying, "Oh, he's friendly, and I'd say courteous, quite chatty in fact." Isabella gave Sophia a curious look, saying, "He did ask about your work and what you would be doing in Brussels!" Sophia responded, "That's right. He did! But what am I supposed to make of it? We can't be suspicious of everyone with a Russian accent, can we?" Nobody responded. Sophia repeated the question. "Well, can we?"

Elsje offered an answer by quietly saying, "Let's talk about this when we get home!" She had noticed the driver glancing, quite often, in the rear-view mirror. Even though there was a sliding glass barrier between the driver and passenger area, he could see everyone. The question was, could he hear everyone as well? Tracey somberly nodded his agreement with the admonition, then pointed toward the ocean saying, "Over there is the Redondo Pier, one of the few remaining California piers. The 'old man', Rowland, and I stopped at the *Bluewater Grill* one time long ago and had hamburgers a person could die for!"

In time, LA drive time, they arrived. The limo pulled up in front of the Schaffer Home on East Ocean Boulevard. Consuelo and Priscilla came out waving. Tracey sighed, saying, "You know, home and bed really are the final frontiers!" Sophia signed for the limo. Elsje told the driver he could place the luggage curbside. "No need to help take things in the house! Thank you!" Elsje kindly insisted. The driver looked disappointed. Or was he irked?

Consuelo, not so politely, bumped the driver as she picked up three bags and hefted them to her side. Then turned and marched toward the house. Consuelo may be a short Mexican woman, but strong as a matched pair of oxen. For reasons developed in times long past, she held a measure of disdain for Europeans.

Cleaning Fair Wind had always been a family affair, except for bottom cleaning, when a diver puts on a wet suit, tanks, and flippers, and cleans algae from the waterline down to the tip of the keel, and the rudder. From the waterline up, the Schaffer family took pleasure in spending a day bringing Fair Wind into the polished beauty she deserved. She was, after all, a 46-foot *Lord Nelson* yacht! Elsje always claimed the interior as her domain.

"Dad! Toss the sponge!" Sophia shouted. She and Isabella were finishing off the cabin top and tying lines at the base of the mast. Tracey was polishing out the stern, the last area to detail before finishing the cleaning. Elsje poked her head up saying, "Don't know about you swabs, but this sailor is hungry! How about dinner at Rang Thongs?"

The four of them agreed. In another hour, they had Fair Wind complete and drove to Rang Thongs, a superb Thai restaurant in Seal Beach. On arrival, they were able to find the last available parking spot. "Sure busy for a Tuesday evening!" Tracey commented.

As they approached the entry, a limo pulled up and stopped. The driver got out to open doors for a group of young people and looked at Elsje and Tracey, and the girls smiled, bowed a little, and said, "Good evening." He was the same man who had driven them home from the airport.

Tracey, Elsje, and the girls paused while the young people piled out, jumping or skipping for the entry, laughing and shouting. It was someone's birthday and they were celebrating in grand style. Instantly, Sophia went to the driver, held out her hand, and while shaking his, said, "I'm Sophia!" then asked, "Where are you from? What is your name?"

The man blushed a little, swept his cap off, and while crunching it in his grip, said, "I am Mykola Kravets. My family is from Lutsk on the Styr River, Ukraine. I grew up there, we had a farm. We milked cows!" His English was barely passable but could be understood well enough. Tracey and Elsje came closer to Mykola. Tracey extended his hand and asked, "What brought you to America?" The man smiled a little, then took on a serious countenance, saying, "I always love America…my cousin too. He lives in Milwaukie. But my family, in Lutsk, they not be so lucky." "How so?" Elsje asked. The man lowered his head, and said, "They are all dead."

"How did they die?" Sophia asked. Mykola looked at Sophia, then Tracey, Elsje, and then Isabella for a moment, then said two words that caused Elsje to take a step back, "Russian Mafia!" Mykola almost whispered the words. But coming from his lips, they sounded like a curse.

"Tracey then asked, "You said you *had* a farm. What happened to it?" Mykola looked at Tracey squarely and said, "They slaughter the herd! Twenty-eight cows they kill. Three dogs, they kill! All our chickens, rabbits, and five pigs, they kill! They burn everything, houses, barns, sheds, tractors, trucks, they burn everything!"

Elsje stepped forward and asked, "Mr. Kravets, how did you escape?" Mykola's face reddened. Tears welled in his eyes. Then, after wiping them with a hankie, said, "I and my friend were hunting. We did not know…we did not know!"

Then Mykola said no more. Put his cap back on, bowed, got back in his limo, and slowly drove away to park and wait. As they walked into the restaurant, Sophia quietly said, "You just never know." No one else said a word. Breaking the uneasy silence, Isobella asked, "Wonder why?" There was no answer. Not a moment passed when Rang Thongs matre d' was there, greeting them by name while escorting the Schaffers to their favorite table.

During dinner, Elsje commented, "We can, with cause, unfortunately, work ourselves into a condition of prejudice. We judge by one category or another. We forget the importance and value of righteous judgment. Which, I suppose, only God truly possesses." Sophia smiled and said, "That's what I was trying to explain when we were being driven home by Mykola from the airport!"

Tracey looked at his daughters and said, "There was a time, not long ago, before you were born, when the entire world was at war. Here in California, and along the entire west coast, Japanese Americans were rounded up and forced into camps to live during the war. Was that righteous judgment? The debate continues! But this I know, when reports of atrocities, inhuman brutalities, and killings, committed against defenseless American, British, and Australian prisoners surfaced in news reports, a very real hatred spread against the Japanese people generally. Was that righteous judgment?" Tracey paused a moment, looked Isabella and Sophia in their eyes, and then quietly said, "I would answer, No! It was categorical, indiscriminate hatred, the same, in context, as Nazi hatred for Jews leading to the institutional slaughter of millions."

Isabella, who does not often engage in conversations of this sort, said, "It is a mystery to me why. Why do people, like those Azra and 'D', and all our family actually, had to defend against, feel compelled to do the things they do?"

Elsje responded, saying, "It is not a mystery if one understands the reality of evil. When it was said that, *'when good people do nothing, evil prevails'*, it was a reminder that battles against evil may be occasionally won, but the war continues. Even though the raid on Bratva, and the Russians, was successful, time will tell when and where the next battle will be engaged. "Why?" Isabella asked. Tracey responded, "Because there are men and women of this world who have lost their ability to weigh right from wrong and have, as Tommy's Yoda doll proclaims, *'chosen the dark side!'*.

The next morning Tracey and Elsje were awakened early. Sophia and Isabella were dressed, had already had a small breakfast, and were anxious to go sailing. "The weather is simply gorgeous! Come on! Get up you lazy heads! Let's get going!" The girls pleaded.

Three hours later Fair Wind passed through the opening to Los Angeles Harbor and was set on a heading that would take them to the far west end of the island. They also agreed to a float plan to sail down the outer side of the island to Cat Harbor. It would be the first place to moor for a couple of nights. Then they would sail to Santa Barbra Island to see the Marine Reserve; then back to Moonstone Cove at Catalina where they would enjoy fresh lobsters tossed into the cockpit by Bruce, the caretaker. Bruce was responsible for collecting mooring fees and checking that sailors observe environmental rules.

"What's this doing aboard?" Tracey asked Sophia. "Well, Dad, I did not think you would mind. I have a special permit to hunt goats with bow and arrow." "What?" Tracey exclaimed, "My daughter is going to kill poor innocent goats!" Tracey put on his best 'deeply offended' face. Then smiled and said, "Well, I suppose it's best if they really intend to eliminate all the goats, that one of the best archers in the country be involved!"

Sophia had brought her *Fred Bear Takedown Recurve* bow, one of the most powerful and beautiful bows ever made. She had applied for and received a permit to harvest three goats on the island. Her championship ribbons went back many years, beginning when she was 12 years old. Most recently, in the 1987 World Archery Championships, in Adelaide, Australia, Sophia took the Silver Medal. Her marksmanship was incredible! Her strength to pull and lose an arrow was amazing, and, her aim was deadly.

Except for rough water near the west end of Catalina, the sail was pleasant. In near record time, they made the turn into Cat Harbor and were soon moored near the seaplane ramp. It was the same mooring Tracey and the old German, Rowland, had taken when they rested that final night before sailing for Hawaii on their intended voyage around the world.

There had been some changes at the Isthmus. Several new cabins had been built plus a small eatery added to the old building, serving exotic foods with a specialty of huge grilled sandwiches. A couple of hikes, with sandwiches for picnics while sitting atop the rocks of Lionhead, at Cherry Cove, and watching some explorer scouts paddling about the cove, made the visit peacefully entertaining. The warm sun, joined with fresh sea breezes slowed time.

The sail to Santa Barbra Island was hurried by a persistent fog-wind foretelling the advance of heavy fog. Just as they arrived at the landing, a thick fog enveloped the Small Island and Fair Wind. The decision was made, practical as it proved to be, to wait the fog out. And, walk across the island, over to Seal Cove, to see the herd of seals gathered there. Two days later the fog lifted and Fair Wind was on its way. But not before circumnavigating the island counterclockwise, as was the Schaffer family tradition.

Back at Catalina Island, the sight of Moonstone Cove was welcomed. The sail had been rough. Wind waves six to eight feet high gave everyone on board a long workout with their legs; constantly adjusting for the pitch and yaw of Fair Wind as they sailed. But Moonstone was as calm and placid as a duck pond. Sheltered from winds and the turbulence it creates on the surface of the sea; Moonstone was a place of solitude for the next five days.

"So, how is it that you can justify killing a little harmless goat?" Isabella casually asked at breakfast. Tracey perked up, put his bagel down, and smiled. It was a pleading smile urging an answer from Sophia. Elsje stopped her galley task and waited.

"We have gone over this before, little sister, they are destroying the vegetation! They eat everything, and soon, if the goat population is not reduced, they will turn this island into a desert!"

"Have you no heart?" Isabella asked.

"Heart? Heart has nothing to do with it! It is a matter of resource management. The same as a forest, or lakes with invasive carp fish, or…"

"Alright girls," Elsje said. Then added, "Enjoy the breakfast and hold the debate later, okay." Tracey looked disappointed that the conversation needed to end.

Sophia quickly finished, went to her berth, and pulled out her bow and quiver of arrows. They were hunting arrows with *Broadhead* points. They had three razor-sharp steel blades at 125 grains. They are the 'takedown' arrow of choice for serious hunting.

After changing into a tight pair of jeans and putting on a red T-shirt, and snake-proof boots for protection, she climbed into the cockpit and whistled, hailing Bruce who was busy checking in a couple of yachts that had just arrived. A few moments later Bruce steered his Boston Whaler over to Fair Wind and hollered, "Going ashore?" Sophia smiled and answered, just loud enough for Isabella to hear, "No! Thought we would chase down a whale and strip it for blubber!"

Sophia shot one goat. A large male with a dynamic set of horns. She tagged it for the Ranger to retrieve. There was a secondary market for trophies which had become quite robust due to the hunt, and the unique character of the Catalina Goat which, evidently, some people like hanging on their walls.

But the sail and puttering around at Moonstone was cut short. There was a call and Tracey needed to get back for a meeting with his Riverside office executive staff. The County planning department, and General staff at March Airforce Base were having arguments which involved land Tracey's firm represented for development for housing Air Force families. "Seems there are environmental concerns over a varmint known as the Kangaroo Rat," Elsje told the girls. Then she chuckled, saying, "Perhaps your father will set up a "Save the Rat" foundation!" "Or create a shoot-the-rats brigade!" Sophia responded. Isabella shook her head and muttered, "How disgusting!"

The sail home was pleasant enough. They crossed paths with the ferry going to Avalon and saw a US Navy Boomer submarine headed west toward the open Pacific Ocean. About halfway through the crossing, they were joined by a dozen dolphins leaping and racing alongside until about six miles out from the entry to Long Beach Harbor and the marina. It had been a good time together. In between the two or three spats over goats or rats, it was a time of solitude. A time for bonding a busy family.

Sophia, anxious to get settled in Brussels, decided to advance her calendar. Isabella needed to use the spare time to check out other offers she had received. One from General Dynamics, and another from Northrop Grumman. And, an interesting career proposal from Fluor Corporation with a starting base salary of $ 320k.

Within a week, everyone is headed in different directions. Sophia is off to work in Brussels. Isabella is back to finishing her master's program at MIT. Rowland and Azra are deeply involved in expanding their fishing and canning business, adding on-shore facilities in Durban, South Africa. And, building a new cannery in Mombasa, Kenya.

Tracey was deeply involved in monitoring the economic effects of several Community General Plans and Urban Growth boundary changes in Riverside, Orange, San Bernardino, and Los Angeles counties. Commercial real estate markets were shifting. On the not-too-distant horizon lurked the advent of internet shopping, of which everyone had an opinion and few if any, understood realities. But one thing was certain; retail, wholesale, and transport of commodities were about to dramatically change.

For Elsje, it was a never-ending struggle to maintain ships, and crews, and meet shipping schedules under international maritime law. Laws that could easily girdle an oceanic shipping company. But the Van Steenwijk Inter-Island Shipping Company has a long, and prestigious history, and was well connected with authorities and governments throughout their service region of the world. With her bags packed, Elsje was off to Jakarta. Consuelo complained, a little, saying, "Too many goodbyes!"

"Mom, I just love this place!" Sophia excitedly voiced over the phone to her mother. "I'm at the Radisson Collection Hotel, at Grand Place, and it is just as sweet as you described. I have looked at a few apartments and will likely get one nearer the Business District! And, A man I met, quite by accident, for we bumped into each other as I was getting into a cab, well he has been a wonderful help. He speaks all the major languages, Dutch, French, German, Flemish, and English, and a little Russian, and, well mom, he is just gorgeous! He drives a Ferrari and is a gentleman of the first order!"

"Does this gentleman have a name? Elsje asked.

"Oh Yes! And, here's the fascinating part, he's from Milan, Italy! His name is Favio Stromboli! Don't you just love it?" Sophia quickly added, "I mean is that not cool or what? And, Mom, he is 6 ft. 4 inches tall. I have to look up at him! And, what a smile!"

"Well, dear, you are a grown woman. Yet to me, being you just turned 23; you are still my baby. Please forgive me if I come off a little restrained."

"I understand Mom. No worries! I know you will just adore Favio when you meet him. I know Dad will as well!" They talked of business for a few moments then said their goodbyes. As she sat the receiver down, Elsje got a strange feeling she could not shake.

Elsje went to bed but could not sleep. As she walked through the kitchen and toward her father's library, which was kept just as it was when he was alive, her maid, Siti, appeared out of the dark and asked if anything was needed. Elsje apologized to Siti who had been with the family ever since she and Tracey were engaged and her maid and dear friend Syahla was killed by Red Turban pirates.

In a flash of revelation or blunt recall of those persistent deadly days, Elsje picked up the phone and called Rowland and Azra. It was not so late, in fact, Elsje reasoned, it was evening in Maputo. "Rowland Schaffer!" Rowland answered. Elsje had become a bit excited and paused, causing Rowland to repeat and ask, "Who is calling?"

"Rowland, dear, this is your mother." Elsje quickly said.

"You sound strange! Is anything wrong?" Rowland asked.

"It's your sister, Sophia…she has met someone!"

"It happens Mom, even to the worst of people, it happens! So, what's the problem, or is there a problem? You sound as if there is…a problem."

"I'm not sure!" Elsje responded. Then added, "Sophia has met this guy and she seems to be all turned on! I just don't have a good feeling about it and no justification for those feelings whatsoever…none!"

"Mom. Calm down. First of all, Heaven help the poor sap if he has garnered Sophia's attention. Second, what do you know of the guy to cause you worries?" Rowland was about to go on but Elsje interrupted, saying, "That's just it, I suppose, I know nothing of him other than a name and that he is Italian, a very handsome Italian according to your sister!"

"Okay, let's start there. What is his name?" Rowland asked.

"Favio Stromboli! And, six foot four inches tall and from Milan!" Elsje responded.

"Do you have a picture?" Rowland asked.

"No, nothing like that," Elsje responded.

"Elsje, this is Azra!

"Oh Azra, I don't mean to sound paranoid but…" Azra interrupted, saying, "It's okay. If you are feeling a mother's concern, then we need to check it out!"

"That is exactly what I am feeling. I had a conversation with Sophia earlier and cannot get this terrible feeling off my back."

"Mom, see if Sophia can get us a picture of the guy!"

"Please do Elsje, then we will contact 'D' who has access to face recognition technology. If there is a problem, she will discover it!" Azra commented.

"Oh, children, bless your hearts! I'll get hold of Sophia tomorrow, or as soon as I can, and ask her for a photograph." Elsje said.

"Careful how you ask mom. You know Sophia!"

"Right! Got it!" Then she added, "Hugs to you both and the kids!"

Two days went by before Elsje and Sophia were able to talk. Sophia had been in back-to-back meetings and Elsje was deeply involved with some warehousing matters in Sri Lanka.

"Hey, mom! How is everything in Jakarta?" Sophia asked over the phone.

"Doing well! How are you dear?" Elsje responded.

"Settling in! Favio helped me find a great apartment and has been a dear helping with getting it furnished. He is so good to me. Even helped select some fantastic artwork. And, I am learning the ropes of the vast markets that exist in Europe for shipping demands to and from Indonesia." Sophia sounded excited and absorbed with her Brussels assignment and, with Favio.

"About Favio, dear, we would love to see a picture of him, to see how handsome your friend is. Could you send one sometime?" Elsje gently inquired.

"Well, Mom, that may be a problem. You see, Favio does not like having his picture taken. He is very conscientious, you see. A little reserved, I'd say!"

"Elsje's nerves tingled a bit but remained calm, saying, "Well, I understand. So, perhaps we will meet Favio someday if you wish?"

"Oh, I'm certain he will want to meet you. Maybe for Christmas and New Year when we all get together in Long Beach!" Sophia responded. Then added, "Rowland and Azra and the kids are coming I hope!"

"As far as we know, they will be there," Elsje responded. Then said, "About Favio, "I'm certain it would be nice to have him come. I am sure he will enjoy meeting your dad, and myself, as well, I would hope."

"Oh Mom, no worries, he'd just love you as I do!" Then she chuckled, "Not certain about Dad. He takes getting used to!" They both laughed, talked about business matters then ended the conversation. As soon as she hung up the phone, Elsje called Tracey. It was the middle of the night. After several rings Tracey groggily answered, saying, "This had better be good!" Elsje responded, "Dearest, it's me. I think we may have a problem!

12

Shutdown

Elsje rehearsed all she knew about Sophia's friend, Favio. The conversation was long, but not too long. Tracey was adamant he should have a talk with Sophia. Elsje was just as adamant that he should wait a few days until she could glean more about the relationship and who Stromboli actually was.

"You know how you and your daughter can sometimes do more of a tangle than tango!" Elsje kindly said.

After a pause, Tracey responded. "Perhaps you're right! I'll wait to hear from you before chatting with our little *Miss Invincible*. But I agree, sweetheart, it would appear we may have a problem, again!" Then, after sweet Adieus, Elsje and Tracey ended the call.

After an hour of tossing and turning, Tracey got out of bed and went to his office. Feeling frustrated, he went to the kitchen, bowed in front of the fridge, and poured a glass of cranberry juice. Back in his office, Tracey leafed through his directory, locating a long-time trusted friend with the FBI. Tracey looked at the clock. It was just past 4:30 am in Washington DC. Anxious yet prudent, Tracey did not make the call and went back to bed. Soon, a needed yet fitful sleep settled him sufficiently to rest.

Several days passed. Tracey was still involved in lengthy hearings over the Kangaroo Rat which somehow had been listed by the government as endangered. Little progress was being made to resolve the matter. At one point, kids with green headbands, waving signs and shouting, held up a dead rat claiming it was "A child of a mourning family!" Tracey started chuckling. When one of the attorneys asked what he was laughing about, Tracey leaned over and whispered, "The government is issuing permits to kill goats on Catalina Island and kids in Riverside County are treating rats like buddies! It's getting insane!" The attorney smiled, leaned back toward Tracey, and whispered, "Just wait until they start demonstrating holding up Rattle Snakes!" "God forbid!" Tracey responded. Then added, "When they do, it's time to find another planet!"

On his way home from one such 'insane' hearing, Tracey received a call from Rowland. Rowland had talked with his sister and was convinced Favio may be an okay guy. "What do you mean by 'may' be a good guy, son?" Tracey inquired.

"Well, Dad, You know me, I'm all details and facts, right? Well, there are a couple of facts missing. First, what does he do for a living? Second, where has he been the past thirty years or so?"

"You said thirty years or so. Did Sophia share his age?" Tracey asked.

"She did. She was hesitant because she thinks you and mom may be concerned that he is seven years plus older than she."

"Well, age does matter in many, not all, relationships. But what is essential to know is who this guy Favio is and what he's all about!" Tracey anxiously exclaimed.

"Look, Dad, I know you and Mom are worried. Just give this thing a little time and it will all shake out!" Rowland responded.

Tracey paused a few seconds, then said, "So long as it doesn't all poop out!"

Rowland laughed, then said, "Love you, Dad! Gotta go!"

Another week passed. There had been no communications from Sophia and Elsje was getting anxious. She was about to call the Brussels office when a FAX document and photograph came into the Jakarta office. It was from Sophia. Elsje's secretary brought it to her saying, "From your daughter in Brussels."

Elsje glanced at the photograph, set it aside, then read the message. "Hi, Mom! Know you are anxious. A friend took this photo of Favio when he and I were at lunch. He did not know. Favio is 31 years old, born in Milan, Italy, and comes from a big wealthy family. He is involved in International Trade Shows all over the world and is on a plane and back all the time. I really admire how well he handles jet lag. Well, we can talk later, Favio and I are doing a concert next week at the La Madeleine. Madonna live! Love, Sophi"

Turning her attention to the photo, Elsje could readily see the attraction, as far as looks went. Favio was very handsome and very young-looking, with an almost innocent look. Then, with a magnifying glass, she looked at his eyes, studying them carefully. Suddenly, Elsje pulled back, laid the magnifying glass down, and caught her breath. What she saw, or thought she saw, was concealment. A look of disguise. A moment later Elsje shook her head and chuckled at herself, whispering aloud, "Worrisome, meddlesome parents!"

But then, that unshakable feeling came over her. Instantly she called her secretary and said, "Please send this to Rowland and Azra in Maputo and my husband. Hurry, please!" The secretary took the documents, glanced at the picture, and said, "Beautiful man!" Then smiled and left the room. Elsje picked up the phone and called Tracey.

"Well, sweetheart, it does not sound or feel good," Tracey responded after hearing the latest. Then he added, "As soon as your fax arrives I'll take a look. And, by the way, I called Frank, you remember him. He's the FBI agent I met and became friends with years ago. Anyway, he is happy to see if they can help. But I think we should let 'D' take the lead on any investigation since she is with Mossad and they are about the best at intelligence!"

"I agree! But it would be good if the FBI could help!" Elsje responded.

"I'm confident they will! However, we need to be our own defenders! You know, they may be good but live in a world of bureaucrats!" Tracey commented. Then added, "Let's see if 'D' discovers anything. Meanwhile, dearest, we need to be vigilant! Right?"

"Right, you are, husband…unfortunately, right you are." Elsje quietly said.

They talked about other matters for a few moments, and then both needed to attend to their work. But not before Elsje said, "Trace, you still have the Old German's Thompson sub-machine gun, perhaps you should give it a cleaning and be certain it's operational. Just in case!"

"Got it! Sweetheart! Will do!" Tracey responded. Then they offered tender adieus with Elsje saying, "When will it all end?" Tracey paused a moment, saying nothing, then quietly said, "Love you!"

A message arrived at the Van Steenwijk office in Jakarta. It was short. "' D' has the photo. Will chase it down!" it was signed, "R". A few days later Tracey was driving toward Newport Beach for a lunch meeting with a client at the Rusty Pelican, situated nicely on the harbor, when a call came on his car phone.

It was 'D" who said, "Hello Mr. Schaffer. I'm afraid I have bad news." Tracey responded, saying, "Give me a second to pull over. Tracey found a beach parking area on Pacific Coast Highway and pulled in. The place was crawling with surfers, swimmers, and picnickers headed for saltwater and sunburns in one of the last good days of early fall!

"Go ahead 'D'! Tracey said.

"We ran the photo, not the best resolution, through face recognition. They have a tentative match. If this guy, Favio, is who we think he is, he's a contract assassin for Bratva and the KGB. He goes by several names, the most common is Favio Stromboli!" 'D's voice was not as clear as one would hope but Tracey got the basics and felt his stomach tighten, his heart pound, and had to roll down the window for some fresh air.

After a few seconds, 'D' shouted, "Tracey, you there?"

"Yes, yes, I'm here!" Tracey responded. Then asked, "Could he be targeting Sophia?"

"We have discussed it and think not! However, he may be using Sophia to gain intelligence on your family, and business activities. But several of our analysts believe the Russians are targeting the best asset you have in terms of Cold War activity!" 'D' said.

Tracey responded, "And what asset may that be?"

"Sorry to say, but it may well be Isabella! Her education and intellect, and her skill-sets in nuclear physics, just may be the prize for ransom in getting what they want from Van Steenwyk Shipping and Rowland and Azra's fishing fleet and canning business in East Africa." 'D' explained.

Tracey was silent for a few seconds, then answered by saying, "If they are right, your analysts, then we may have a more serious problem than thought." Then he asked, "Forget the analyst's view, what do you think?"

'D' came right back, saying, "All things considered, I believe it's Isabella!"

Tracey paused again, then said, "We need to get organized! We need a plan. Are you in a position to help?"

'D' responded, "Absolutely, but first, we need to confirm this guy Favio and I need your permission to have our Mossad unit in Brussels check this out. And, understand, we have him, if it is him, on our target list as well!"

"Everyone has a 'target list' these days! Even goats are targets!" Tracey mumbled.

"What! What was that about goats?" 'D' shouted.

"Never mind! Not important. And, yes, do what you need to do to check this Favio Stromboli out and keep us informed!"

"We are on it! Talk soon!" 'D' said. Then, except for static, there was silence.

Tracey sat there, among a throng of beach-goers, all happy, carefree, and seeking the pleasures of sun, sand, and surf. As he observed, he felt an impression swell in his heart. A swelling carrying simple refrains of freedom and what it means to be an American. After a few more moments, Tracey recaptured the realities of conditions besetting him and his family, started his Mercedes, and raced for Newport Beach. On the way, he called Elsje. When she answered, it was obvious she too had been sound asleep. She did not hesitate to mimic her husband by saying, "This had better be good!". Tracey responded, "Well, sweetheart, I so wish it were, but it's not!"

Tracey quickly rehearsed what he learned from 'D'. Elsje responded, "Dear husband, watch your driving! Do your lunch meeting! Then, dear, call me in about four hours. We shall talk then!" Tracey hung up his phone and drove toward the Rusty Pelican. His mind spun hundreds of what-ifs, the Thompson sub-machine gun, and Isabella, and Sophia. He was so tempted to call her, Sophia, right then but instead focused on crazed PCH drivers!

That evening, Tracey and Elsje connected. "I know this sounds a little off-key but it may be best for 'D' to relate the bad news to Sophia." Elsje quietly said.

"She's our daughter! We love her! And, we have a responsibility as parents for her safety! Do we not?" Tracey retorted.

"All true! No question dear. But, please listen to me, when it comes to Sophia, acceptance of truth can be rejected because of misunderstood intentions. You know how independent she is, how we have openly admired and encouraged it. But when it comes to a relationship with a man she, as an adult, has developed or is nurturing, well, her independence quotient will be at the extreme. We may know a sad and dangerous truth! However, this Favio is likely skilled enough to turn whatever we say on its head, into malicious meddling! What then of Sophia's reaction? What then of the outcome?"

Tracey did not respond for a few seconds. Then, calmly, he said, "You know, that's what I love about you. You measure critical situations so incredibly well!"

"Is that the ONLY reason you love me?" Elsje laughingly responded.

"Only one among all the reasons any man could ever hope for!" Tracey softly said. Then added, "I'll get hold of 'D' and ask. I'm certain she will handle it well.

"Good!" Elsje responded. Then said, "I'm going to call Isabella and see how she is doing. Take care, darling. Talk soon!"

The next day, after several attempts, Tracey was able to talk with 'D'. After explaining what Elsje had said, related to parenting, 'D' agreed and said she would handle the matter, saying, "I am sending two Mossad agents from our Brussels unit, Rebecca and David, to visit Sophia. They are already on queue to observe them at the Madonna concert, which is tomorrow evening. They will likely follow them, and then talk with Sophia when the timing is right. I'll let you know!" Then she quickly added, "I would suggest you get the girls home as soon as you can. I have a plan that I'll explain later.

After a gracious salutation of appreciation, Tracey sent Elsje a fax message to the Van Steenwijk home. Twenty minutes later, a fax came back with a short note and a kiss mark at the bottom. Right after the word "PERSERVERE!"

The next afternoon, Pacific Daylight Time, Tracey received a call at his Newport Beach office. When he answered, he recognized it was Sophia. But she was crying and coughing. A moment later, after Tracey assured her he was listening, Sophia said, "Oh Dad, how could I have been so stupid! Stupid, stupid, stupid!"

Calmly, Tracey responded, "Listen carefully, sweetheart. It is not you who is the stupid one. It's Favio and his employers. They are incredibly stupid to believe they can compromise one of my children to advance their evil designs!" Then Tracey added, "I'm certain the Mossad agents related all they could?"

"Yes, Dad. More than I wanted to hear! He's married, dad…married! And, dad, he has three children! Arrrrggg!" Sophia shouted.

"Likely more, but not all by the same woman!" Tracey quipped.

Then Sophia said something any true father would hope to hear when she said, "Well, there is nothing to fear about that not-so-little problem with me. He tried but I kept the virtues you and Mom taught me, Dad. No worries about that!" Then Sophia repeated her "Stupid" self-condemnation. Then, she said, "You know, after I showed him a picture of Isabella, he began wanting to know all about her. At first, I felt a little jealous, you know sister stuff, but when he seemed more interested in her education and who she may work for, I thought it was more of a professional-related inquiry. He certainly made it sound legitimate!

"Look sweetheart, your mom and 'D' and I have discussed this, a lot, and feel it is time to shut down Bratva. They are planning a play for Isabella, likely an abduction. Your mom will be calling soon and we want all our children here as soon as possible. If they need a target, we're going to give them one. So get packed and wait for your mother's call. And dear daughter, I love you so very much." Tracey slowly hung up. Then stood there, looking out toward the ocean, seeing Catalina far in the distance. He smiled, feeling the energy of a father's pride, the comfort of a daughter's love.

The practicality of matters prevented immediate action for the girls to return to Long Beach. Isabella needed to complete a few critical details for her thesis review. Sophia had several meetings to attend and was doing her best to carefully cool the Favio relationship. Thanksgiving was but three days away and holiday mode was setting in with all the commercial enticements corporate marketeers could conjure!

Finally, Isabella and Sophia confirmed they could be home the Saturday following Thanksgiving. The best and safest solution for getting the girls home was for Sophia to fly to Boston and join Isabella there. Elsje flew from Jakarta to Long

Beach in the Van Steenwijk jet, then sent it on to Boston where Sophia and Isabella would be met.

Due to flight scheduling from Brussels, Sophia would need to room with Isabella overnight. Arrangements were made for them to be transported to Boston International Airport and then board the jet at *Signature Flight Support,* a secure corporate and private aircraft facility where the pilot and co-pilot would be waiting.

All went well. That Saturday afternoon, at about 4:30 pm, Tracey and Elsje watched the Gulfstream 600 gently land at Long Beach International Airport and taxi to the *Signature Flight Support* facility at Daugherty Field. A few moments later, with hardly a word said, grateful parents and glad daughters embraced and kissed each other.

In the car, however, there was a deluge of questions, most asked by Isabella who had not yet fully realized the danger she was in. Elsje turned to Isabella saying, "The summation is this, the Russians are attempting a strategic move to control vast regions of the planet. Indonesia and East Africa are two primary targets. They need to infiltrate by taking over certain industries. Transportation and food production are but two. Van Steenwijk Shipping and Rowland and Azara's fishing fleet and canning operations appear to be their primary objective. And, the method they are using is to extort our businesses through abduction and forced compliance. And, sweetheart, we have discovered you are the one they now want to abduct, having failed to get what they want by taking Teressa and Tommy!"

"Where are Rowland and Azra in this terrible game?" Sophia asked.

"They are on their way here and will arrive in two days, Monday morning, here at Long Beach!" Tracey responded.

 "Why are we all gathering here?" Isabella asked.

Elsje answered, saying, "'D' and your dad and I, and Mossad strategists, have determined to make ourselves a target. We know that they know what we are doing. Somehow, they are tracking every move we make. So, we are here for the holidays, celebrating as normal. And, we will take a traditional family sail to Catalina, Moonstone Cove, where we will set the trap and shutdown Bratva!"

"With help from the FBI!" Tracey added.

"How can we help?" Sophia asked. "Yes, how can we help?" Isabella repeated.

Tracey responded, "You, Miss Champion archer, can bring your bow and arrows! And, you sweetheart, can stay close to your mom and be watchful! "Oh good!" Isabella quipped, "I don't have to shoot anything!" Tracey and Elsje looked at each other. Elsje smiled and looking at Isabella, said, "Just stay close by sweetheart."

Azra and Rowland arrived on schedule. "I miss the kids!" Elsje commented on the way to the car. "Best they stay with Adelia in Maputo until we get this done," Azra responded.

The marine air had become thick, and wet, moving swiftly along the Long Beach shore, and inland. By the time they arrived at the Schaffer residence, it was total fog. Vision was reduced to less than a city block distance. Nonetheless, Consuello and Priscilla were waiting just outside the garage.

Ready, as always, to lend a hand with luggage or whatever needed to be done. Both girls gave Consuelo and Priscilla hugs.

During the late Thanksgiving dinner that evening, details of the plan were laid out. It was quite simple really. The family, which included Rowland and Azra, would sail to Catalina and take a mooring at Moonstone Cove. Mossad would monitor movements by Bratva and the KGB, keeping the family informed through 'D". The FBI would provide four special operations personnel, a lead agent, and a helicopter which would be staged at Long Beach Airport and engage when events develop to warrant their assistance. The rest was up to Bratva and whatever they may be planning to do.

"So, I'm the goat, staked for slaughter?" Isabella commented.

"And a lovely one at that!" Tracey responded.

"So, are we supposed to just sit and wait?" Sophia asked.

"That could never happen!" Rowland chuckled. "You two are like the perpetual bouncing ball!

"Well, look who is talking!" Isabella quipped.

Elsje intervened, saying, "We will do what we have always done as a family. Enjoy the water, swim, go shell hunting, have wonderful meals, sing and tell awful boring stories to each other!" Elsje smiled and took a posture that she had said her piece.

Sophia would not let a chance pass and mumbled, "Dad tells the worst!" Azra protested saying, "I love his stories!" They laughed as Tracey shook his head in agreement with both points of view.

Their conversation shifted to each other's progress in work and studies, business and pleasure, and other family members, especially Terresa and Tommy who would stay with Adelia until safe to come to Long Beach. And, it was learned, as Sophia related more about Favio that she had revealed much about Isabella's studies; where she lived, where she may work, even shared pictures.

By the end of the first week in December, Fair Wind was loaded for the crossing to Catalina. The weather was warmer than normal. The Eastern Pacific high-pressure bubble had drifted farther east and was sitting atop the region. But there was sufficient breeze to sail, be it even a slow sail, no one would complain.

'D' called relating that several Bratva agents and one known KGB woman were spotted in Los Angeles. All indications were they would make the abduction attempt at either the Schaffer Home or at Catalina Island. She confirmed that it would be a more controlled environment at Catalina. She also said that Mossad and the FBI were coordinating. Then said, "I so wish I could be there! It would please me no-end to catch Lev!"

Tracey asked, "Do you have confirmation their leader, Lev, is here?"

One of our agents says he's certain one of the Bratva goons in LA is Lev. But we have not been able to confirm! Will let you know if and when we do!"

That next morning, Tracey and Elsje gathered the family together and had a moment of prayer. Tracey asked for God to protect them, their home, and Fair Wind, and help them put an end to the pestilence that has plagued them for so long. Then off to the marina and sail to Moonstone Cove.

As expected, the sail was slow. The typical four-hour crossing took nearly five hours. But, as they picked up the mooring wand and secured lines, fore and aft, it was absolutely beautiful. The Garibaldi fish were everywhere. The water was smooth and crystal clear. And, just as Rowland and Azra were getting into the dingy, named "Thumper", they heard two or three goats bleating. Rowland hollered, "Hey sisters, your friends are waiting!" Both Sophia and Isabella responded with bleats of their own making. "Well done…well done!" Rowland quipped. By then Elsje had her swimsuit on and dived into the water. Right after, Rowland plunged in and swam for the beach, racing after Rowland and Azra.

When they arrived, there were five yachts in the cove. Three days later, there were twelve. With the weekend coming, there would likely be a full cove, keeping Bruce, the cove manager, busy putting about on his Boston Whaler with twin Yamaha 50 engines. Bruce was a speedy kind of guy and loved tinkering with mechanical stuff!

By Friday night the cove was nearly full. The weather, even though it was early December, was delightful with near-perfect temperatures, around 76 degrees. The next day the Schaffers were lazy about getting up. There had been dew during the night and the cabin top was still wet. But the air was warming and turning dry. Elsje had the binoculars out looking around the cove and out to sea. While looking toward the far end, she paused, taking a second look at a low-profile yacht. It was a boat designed for speed and not for relaxing.

Tracey was not quite awake. Elsje went to the berth and said, "Think you had best take a look at a new tenant in the cove!"

Tracey finished pulling up blue jeans, slipped a Maui volcanic mud-stained T-shirt over his head, and followed Elsje up into the cockpit. After clearing his eyes, Tracey leveled the binoculars on the boat and watched for the longest time. Then quietly said, "Looks like no one is on board." Elsje responded, "I know, but it sure looks out of place for Moonstone!"

Just then Tracey said, "Wait! I see someone. No, three guys! No, there are two more, I see five men and they do not look like sailors or vacationers!" Tracey put down the binoculars and went below. On the VHF radio, he called Bruce who, after three attempts, answered. Tracey asked if he had checked in a vessel at the far end of the cove. Bruce came back, saying, "Not yet! They came in early this morning, around 4:00 am. Been over here at Whites Landing working on my cart!" Then Bruce asked, "Is there a problem?"

Tracey responded, "Just curious, perhaps nothing!"

Bruce called back, saying, "Be back in an hour or so. Will check it out Mr. Schaffer, No worries!"

Tracey turned to Elsje and asked, "Where is Isabella?"

"Not sure! Thought she was still asleep!"

Tracey went to where the girls berthed. Sophia was just waking up but Isabella was not there. Tracey turned toward the head and knocked. No response. Then opened the door but it was empty. Looking around the cabin and seeing no one but Rowland and Azra who were stirring, he climbed back into the cockpit and whispered, "Isabella is gone!"

Elsje looked toward shore with the binoculars and exclaimed, "There she is, way down the beach. She appears to be looking for moonstones." Then added, "Here, have a look." Tracey took the binoculars, steadied them, and confirmed it was Isabella, toward the far end of the cove. The dingy, Thumper, was sitting on the beach some one hundred yards back toward where Fair Wind was moored. Then Tracey shifted his gaze toward the vessel with five men and saw four boarding a rubber skiff, getting ready to paddle ashore.

Tracey yelled toward Isabella. But she was too far away to hear. His throat tightened, and his gut winched as he said, "Good God! I think it's Bratva!" Elsje grabbed the VHF and called for Bruce. Instantly he responded. Elsje yelled, "Come quick, emergency! Come quick Bruce!" Bruce responded, "On my way!"

Tracey grabbed the satellite phone and called the number he was given for the FBI special operations team. There was a garbled answer. Static interference scrambled his words and any words coming back. He went back to the cockpit and took the binoculars from Elsje who ran below to wake Rowland and Azra, saying but one word, "Bratva!" In a flash Azra and Rowland were dressed and into the cockpit. Tracey turned to Rowland saying, "Get the Thompson!" Without a word, Rowland dashed back below, grabbed the Thompson submachine gun, and jammed a magazine into place.

Sophia came up with her bow and quiver of arrows. Azra went back below and brought up the rest of their firearms. Elsje screamed toward Isabella. But still, she could not hear. Rowland looked over the side and shouted, "Where's Thumper?"

Traccy responded, "Isabella went ashore. It's with her. Here, have a look." Rowland gazed through the binoculars and upon spotting Isabella, caught the edge of the rubber skiff being aggressively rowed by two of the men. Rowland threw down the binoculars, jumped up on the gunnels, and dove in shallow. He surfaced and swam as hard as he could for the beach some fifty yards distant.

Just then, the rumble of Bruces' Boston Whaler could be heard and in seconds he was next to Fair Wind and yelled, "What's going on?"

"Serious trouble!" Tracey yelled back as he jumped in Bruces's boat with the Thompson in hand.

"Jeepers! Mr. Schaffer. What's the gun for?"

Tracey, in a growling tone, said, "Get this hot rod of yours down to that boat that came in early this morning and you'll find out!"

As they pulled away, Tracey yelled back saying, "Keep trying to get the FBI!"

As with all boats moored at Catalina coves, it was tethered bow out toward the sea. The Boston Whaler was near full throttle and made the end of the cove in seconds. As they passed the last two yachts, before getting to the boat carrying the five men, the one left on board came forward and fired two shots but missed. Bruce instantly swerved and pulled back on the throttle. Tracey raised the Thompson and fired a burst at the man who screamed as he flew off into the water. Then Tracey fired another burst at the bow, aiming just below the waterline. The sleek power boat instantly began to settle deeper into the water.

"Get around this piece of junk and head for the beach!" Tracey growled. Bruce jammed the throttle forward and the Whaler lurched toward shore. As soon as he could get a clean view, Tracey saw that the men had Isabella who had apparently run toward a line of eucalyptus trees and was headed back toward the rubber skiff. Tracey raised up and fired a burst, hitting the skiff several times, causing it to fold like a soggy newspaper and sink into the surf.

The men fired back, hitting the Boston Whaler several times but missing Bruce and Tracey. Bruce backed up and spun the Whaler around to get behind the sinking vessel the men had come on. The four men turned and began running up a trail toward the hilltop leading to White's Landing. "They are headed for White's! I can get you there fast!" Bruce yelled.

"Get us back to Fair Wind first!" Tracey yelled.

Bruce pushed the throttle forward. As they roared between the moored vessels and the beach, people were out gawking, hollering questions about what was happening. Spotting Rowland, who had made the beach and was retrieving Thumper, Tracey yelled, "Get back to the boat and stay with your mom!" Rowland waved and shook his head that he understood.

As they approached Fair Wind, Tracey yelled, "Azra, Sophia, jump in!" Azra jumped in with Sophia close behind. Azra had two weapons, the 12-gauge sawed-off shotgun and a Beretta. Sophia had her bow and quiver of arrows.

"They may be headed for the airport!" Bruce yelled.

"How would they get there?" Azra asked.

"Carts, golf carts. It's the only way to get around on the island!" Bruce shouted back. Then added, "There are several at White's, including mine!" He turned and tossed a set of keys to Tracey yelling, "You can't miss it. It's candy apple red with white pin stripping a raked roof and bigger rear wheels. And has a gas engine, a go-cart engine that is superpowered! Fastest cart on the island! Hell, perhaps the planet!" Bruce paused a few seconds as he navigated close to rocks at the point rounding into White's Landing. Then yelled again, "If you really, I mean really need speed, just push the button marked 'OD' and hang on!" He chuckled, then focused on getting to the jetty at the far end.

Azra called out, "There! There they are!" Tracey and Sophia looked and could see Isabella being held by her hair as they boarded two golf carts. Azra exclaimed, "The man holding Isabella is Lev. Head of Bratva!" As Bruce continued steering toward the jetty the two golf carts took off up the twisting dirt road toward the airport. Lev, Isabella, and one of the Bratva goons were in the lead cart. The other two goons followed with automatic weapons at the ready.

The tide was out making it a ladder climb to the top of the jetty. Once there, Tracey, Azra, and Sophia ran for the building where, under an overhead shade structure, a candy apple red, beastly-looking, golf cart sat. At that moment, Bruce shouted, "Don't hurt my baby, 'The Red Devil'!" "What was that?" Tracey asked. Azra shrugged her shoulders saying, "Something about a baby, and a devil, I think." Tracey got a queer look on his face, then mumbled, "Kids! You just never know!"

Tracey jammed in the key, turned it, and whooom! The cart was purring. Purring like a roadster sitting at a drag race starting line! Tracey was totally surprised and carefully put it into gear. In a cloud of dust, they were off, trailing far behind the other two carts but would quickly close the gap.

"Watch the curves!" Sophia shouted.

"I've got this!" Tracey shouted back. Sophia rolled her eyes, gave a slight smile to Azra, then took a better grip. Azra smiled back. Then when the cart spun around a sharp curve and nearly went up on two wheels, took a better grip herself.

Within moments they were eating dust from the carts ahead of them. "Best not get too close! "Azra shouted.

"Can't see a damn thing. Don't know how close or far we are from the boogers!" Tracey shouted back.

Just then, a burst of shots came flying past the Red Devil. Tracey swerved and almost lost control. Around another two curves, they could barely see the cart ahead. It was there, then gone in the dust cloud. Another curve and more shots. All were wild. Azra shouted, "I can't shoot back! No way of knowing where Isabella is!" Tracey, both hands tight on the wheel, head down and squinting through the dust, just nodded.

Then, all of a sudden, a puff of wind revealed the cart ahead. It was just about to disappear around a curve when out of nowhere something dark, and huge, came flying off the upper bank, and WHAAM! Whatever it was slammed into the cart. The two goons went flying into the air above the dust, followed by the cart which sailed over the edge of the embankment. Tracey had just enough time to slam on the brakes. The dust cloud drifted just enough to see a huge male goat with a vicious set of horns, what had to be the patriarch of the Catalina Goat Kingdom, standing, snorting, looking down the bank.

A few seconds later two additional large male goats with monster horns ran to his side. Together, the three goats looked down for a few seconds then leaped over the edge. Tracey jammed the cart in gear and raced forward. Then slammed on the brakes, stopped, and jumped out for a quick look. Down about fifty feet were the two goons being hammered by three goats. Worse, the goons had landed in a patch of prickly pear. It was a sight to behold. Tracey threw his arms into the air, and waved them back and forth, yelling, "Yahoo! Goats two…Russians Zero! YAHOO!" Then in a more somber tone, Tracey whispered, "Providential!"

"Dad, got to go!" Sophia shouted. Tracey jumped in, threw the cart in gear, and took off. Then yelled back at Sophia asking, "What was that Bruce said about going faster?" "It's the 'OD' button Dad…but he…" Sophia couldn't finish. Tracey hit the 'OD' button and the front wheels reared up, and the rear wheels spun, kicking dirt and rocks out the back like a machine gun! Then Sophia slowly finished, saying, "But he said hold on!" The Red Devil was screaming faster and faster. Tracey was barely able to hold it to the ground around curves without spinning out!

A few moments later, dust from the lead cart, with Isabella cloaked Tracey, Azra, and Sophia. After a few moments more they were near the airport. Azra spotted a small terminal building with clusters of trees nearby. She also spotted a plane sitting on the tarmac with its side door open. It was a Cessna 420 Golden Eagle!

Tracey yelled, "When I stop, you two head for those trees and do what you can. I'll get as close as I can and see what can be done to stop the plane." Azra and Sophia nodded their understanding and braced themselves. Azra hoisted the shotgun and checked her holstered Beretta. Sophia slung her bow over one shoulder and fastened the quiver about her waist.

Seconds later Tracey pulled over to a near stop. Azra and Sophia leaped out, running toward the trees. In that same instant shots rang out. Sophia got the first clean look and realized the man shooting was Favio. His first shots were at Tracey. Tracey had stopped the cart and fired a burst at the plane's front wheel. Instantly the tire blew apart. Tracey then pointed toward Favio and pulled the trigger. But the Thompson sub-machine gun jammed. Favio raised his pistol, walked briskly toward Tracey, and was about to pull the trigger when an arrow sliced into his left ear and protruded out of his right ear. Favio spun around nearly twice with the force of the arrow and collapsed dead.

Lev and Isabella were at the steps entering the plane. A woman appeared at the door, raised an Ozzi, and was about to fire, when she was blown away by the 12-gauge Azra was holding. Sophia had her bow readied and walked toward Lev, still holding Isabella by the hair. Suddenly, Lev held a pistol at Isabella's head and threatened, with a curse, that he would kill her if they didn't back away. Tracey had cleared the jam but stopped. Azra stopped as well but held the shotgun pointed directly at the pilot who had his hands in the air, like anxiously holding up the ceiling of the plane's cockpit.

Softly, Azra said to Sophia, "Got him?" Sophia, just as calmly responded, "Yep!"

Lev was attempting to back up the steps, holding Isabella in front of him. Sophia had moved slightly to her right for a better angle. Then, just as the rather plump, short, and definitely unsightly leader of the Russian Mafia called Bratva took another step, exposing his bum. It was just enough for Sophia to let the arrow fly. The scream was nearly frightening as Lev went to the ground, face down, bum raised high with the arrow pinning both cheeks of his flabby buttocks together!

Isabella reached down, picked up Lev's gun, and pointed it at his head. Tracey, Azra, and Sophia froze. Then after a few tense seconds, Isabella pointed the gun at the other two tires. With a series of rapidly fired shots, they too were blown away.

Not two seconds later, a black helicopter with FBI markings suddenly appeared and dropped down on the tarmac. Special ops guys came out and quickly surrounded the plane. One leaped inside to check things out and dragged the pilot out by his neck.

The FBI lead agent came to where Tracey, Azra, and the two sisters, holding each other close, were standing. He nodded to Tracey, looked down at Lev, leaned over, and in Russian said, "Oh my, that looks like a world of hurt! You're going to need loads of help going potty for a very long time!" Then he turned to his special ops guys, saying "When you've figured a way to get this piece of trash hauled out of here…well, get it done!"

After a brief conversation with the FBI agent, Tracey, Azra, Sophia, and Isabella, climbed on The Red Devil and headed back down the winding dirt road to White's Landing. On the way they stopped, looked over the bank, and gazed at two very broken and dead Russian Mafia goons lying in a prickly pear patch. Nobody spoke for a moment. Then Isabella calmly said, "Suppose they will need to figure a way to transport that trash as well!"

Bruce was anxiously waiting. As Tracey pulled the cart up to the shelter, Bruce asked if everyone was okay. But while asking, performed a detailed inspection of his "baby". Pleased to find no bullet holes Bruce turned, smiled, and said, "I'll get you folks home to Fair Wind, if I may?" Tracey reached out, placed a hand on Bruce's shoulder, and said, "That's the wildest golf cart I've ever drivin'! Don't think it would do all that well at the Country Club though!"

The ride back to Moonstone Cove was gentle. And quiet. Soon they pulled up next to Fair Wind where Elsje and Rowland were waiting. Elsje embraced Tracey, then her daughter Isabella. Then Sophia and Azra. Rowland then said,

"Sounded like a war. We could hear the shooting. It echoed everywhere."

Tracey looked around the cove, then asked, "Where did all the yachties go?" The cove had only five yachts moored and one sunken speed boat at the far end. A pile of rubber, which was once a skiff, lay on the beach. Tracey then looked at everyone and humbly said, "We survived. And we have God to thank." Then added, "What say we head home?" Everyone nodded in agreement and went about sailor's tasks to prepare Fair Wind for an afternoon sail across the Channel, and home. The wind was up. About 18 knots. Perfect for Fair Wind to show her stuff, sails full and tight.

As they departed Moonstone, the western sky took on a soft amber glow, confirming the sun had long passed its apex. For a short distance, Bruce cruised alongside, then put his Whaler in neutral, and waved goodbye. Just as he was waving, they heard a goat bleat from somewhere up on the hill. It was a deep, manly sort of bleat. The bleat of a patriarch goat? Everyone, in their own way and pitch or tone, returned the bleat. Tracey repeated his earlier comment, "Providential!" In unison, they echoed his salutation.

During the crossing, Elsje called 'D' on the satellite phone. "We watched every detail on our sky-spy system!" 'D' exclaimed. Then added, "Incredible! But the imagery was not clear when those two, along with the cart, went flying! What was that all about?"

"A grandpa goat and his buddies took out the cart, and Russians!" Tracey replied.

"Divine intervention?" 'D' commented.

"What else!" Elsje responded with a smile.

"You got Lev! You got the prize! And saved Isabella! You guys are incredible! We are all so very happy for you."

"Thank you! And please thank everyone at Mossad for all you have done. You made it possible!" Elsje commented.

It was nearly dark when they arrived at Long Beach Marina. After stowing things and checking to see that Fair Wind was secure, the family left for home. Two days later Adelia arrived with Terresa and Tommy. There was just enough time to prepare for the traditional combined celebration of Hanukkah and Christmas and was a complete and beautiful surprise when the doorbell rang and there stood 'D'. As she was warmly greeted, 'D' said "Well, I just couldn't miss this occasion. They let me loose for a few days and I just had to see the kids!" A cab driver, standing behind her, cleared his throat to garner attention. Attention as to what to do with a stack of gifts he was carrying.

The celebration began. At dusk, a simple dinner of potato cakes and other Jewish dishes was placed on the table. The first of seven Hanukkah candles was lit. "I want to propose a toast!" Tracey announced. Everyone took their glasses and stood. "To Conquest, Mossad, our Navy Seals, CIA, and FBI, and all who so generously and expertly aided in the fight against such vile evil. To 'D', to Adelia, and her beloved Eka, who is with God, their daughter, the *Lioness of Gaza*, and, my beautiful Elsje, and children, May God be with you, always!" A cheer resounded. Consuelo and Pricilla lifted a glass and all applauded.

Christmas was celebrated with attendance at a Christmas Concert, a tour of Naples Island homes ablaze with holiday lights, and, most traditionally, watching the Christmas Boat Prade in Alamitos Bay. Tracey and Elsje watched from the bridge railing as gondolas, yachts, and a trail of Sabots filled with kids, all beautifully decorated, floated slowly by. Tracey leaned over, kissed Elsje gently on her cheek, and whispered, "It is over!" Elsje quietly responded, "And that, dear husband, is the best Christmas gift ever!

THE END